Such polite conversation

They were doing famously—even if Eve was barely breathing. She smiled, searching for a line to facilitate her escape.

"Do you know what day it is?" Parker asked before she managed it.

She felt her heart turn over. There was only one reason for him to ask that question. "Friday," she said evenly.

"August the seventeenth." He held her gaze, his eyes dark and intent. "Our wedding day," he added.

"We didn't have a wedding day."

"No, you're right, we didn't have one." His voice was oddly expressionless. She clenched her hands by her side. She steeled herself against the memories.

Eve was shaking. She had to get away from Parker, from the terrifying emotions coursing through her....

KAREN van der ZEE is an author on the move. Her husband's work as an agricultural adviser to developing countries has taken them to many exotic locations. The couple said their marriage vows in Kenya, celebrated the birth of their first daughter in Ghana and their second in the U.S., where they make their permanent home. The whole family spent two fascinating years in Indonesia. Karen has had several short stories published in her native Holland, and her modern romance novels with their strong characters and colorful backgrounds are enjoyed around the world.

Books by Karen van der Zee

HARLEQUIN PRESENTS
982—FANCY FREE
1126—SHADOWS ON BALI
1158—HOT PURSUIT
1222—BRAZILIAN FIRE
1350—JAVA NIGHTS
1422—KEPT WOMAN

HARLEQUIN ROMANCE
2334—SWEET NOT ALWAYS
2406—LOVE BEYOND REASON
2652—SOUL TIES

KAREN
VAN DER ZEE

the imperfect bride

Harlequin Books

TORONTO • NEW YORK • LONDON
AMSTERDAM • PARIS • SYDNEY • HAMBURG
STOCKHOLM • ATHENS • TOKYO • MILAN
MADRID • WARSAW • BUDAPEST • AUCKLAND

Harlequin Presents first edition August 1992
ISBN 0-373-11486-9

Original hardcover edition published in 1991
by Mills & Boon Limited

THE IMPERFECT BRIDE

CHAPTER ONE

Eve waded out of the water on to the beach, aware that the little boy was watching her. She was used to people watching her, although usually the adults tried to pretend they didn't notice the funny way her left leg dragged.

She smiled at him, but as soon as he realized she knew he was looking he turned abruptly and kicked his ball across the soft powdery sand. Obviously he'd been told not to stare at people, but just for a moment he'd forgotten.

He was alone on the beach, but as long as he didn't go into the water by himself he was safe enough. The rocky cove with its beautiful crescent of white coral sand was the private property of the Plantation, a small, exclusive island resort where the rich and famous escaped the burdens of celebrity.

Eve stretched out on her mat, picked up her book and tried to concentrate. A few minutes later something touched her foot, and she looked up to find the soccer ball in the sand beside her.

The boy came running over and picked it up hastily. "Sorry I bothered you," he said politely. He looked at her guiltily, twirling the ball between his small tanned hands.

Eve felt an odd shock as she looked into the earnest brown eyes. Her stomach tightened. She tried to smile. "No problem."

She swallowed. She recognized those brown eyes, the solemn look. No, it couldn't be. Her imagination was working overtime. Millions of people the world over had serious brown eyes.

"You like reading?" he asked, his gaze fixed on her book. His black hair was thick and springy—just like Parker's.

She nodded. "I do, but this book is a little difficult. I should have brought something fun for the beach." *Sensory Processing in the Child*. Not exactly the type of literature normally read at the beach of an idyllic Caribbean island where the trade winds gently stirred the palm fronds and turquoise waters sparkled in the sun.

"My dad reads to me every night before I go to bed," the boy told her. "I can read myself, too. My dad says reading is very important. He says if you can't read well you're handicap...ped." His face turned a deep red. His eyes glanced away.

"Handicapped isn't a dirty word," Eve said gently.

"I'm sorry," he muttered, painfully embarrassed. "I didn't mean to..."

"Of course not." Eve smiled reassuringly. "I am handicapped—I know that. Everybody can see it. It's not an insult, you know, it's just the way it is."

He let out a deep sigh, then dropped like a rag in the sand. "I thought you'd be angry."

"No. You weren't trying to be mean, so I'm not angry." The same determined chin. The same tilt to his head when he talks. Please God, let me be wrong.

He sighed again. "Good." He glanced at her leg. "Don't you mind? About your leg, I mean?"

"Oh, I mind, of course. I'd much rather have two good legs rather than one. But I can walk, and I'm very, very lucky."

His eyes widened. "Lucky?" He seemed unable to conceive of the possibility, and Eve smiled.

"I was in a very bad car accident—I could have died. I could have been sitting in a wheelchair now. When I think of that, I can only feel very lucky."

"Yeah." He looked at her bare left leg, eyeing the scars, the odd shape of it. "Does it hurt?"

"In the beginning it hurt a lot, but not any more. Only when I'm very tired it hurts a little." She smiled. "What's your name?"

"Joshua."

"I like that. It's a good name." She wished he'd told her his last name, but didn't want to ask for it. "How old are you?"

"Eight. I'm going into third grade in September."

Five years ago Parker's son had been three. Her hands tensed, fingers digging into the sand. It couldn't be. It couldn't be! It would be too much of a coincidence. Why the Plantation? Why not the Malliouhana on Anguilla? Or Jumby Bay on Petit St. Vincent? There were other hideaway resorts in the Caribbean, why the Plantation?

"Are you on vacation with your parents?" she asked.

He nodded. "With my dad and my aunt Janey and my grandma and grandpa. My dad has to work, though, but sometimes I can go with him." He jumped up. "Aunt Janey's here. We're gonna go swimming now. Bye!" He raced off, kicking up the sand.

Aunt Janey was young and pretty. Eve watched the tall, slim figure emerge from the shadowy fringe of coconut palms. She stepped lightly through the soft white sand, moving with the elegance of a ballet dancer. She wore a simple sky-blue swimsuit and had a shiny cap of curly, honey-colored hair.

Eve felt a wave of pain so severe, it shocked her. Where was that coming from so suddenly? Five years was a long time.

Joshua, if he was Parker's son, had no mother; she had died when Joshua was three. Maybe Aunt Janey was Joshua's stepmother, Parker's wife.

Eve stared blindly at her book, the words nothing but a blur. This was crazy! Joshua was just a little boy with dark hair and brown eyes, the son of a Broadway producer or an incognito politician or some other lofty personality taking refuge on the Plantation. Somebody else's son, not Parker's.

She watched him now as he helped his aunt spread out two mats, and she could hear them laugh. The next moment they raced each other to the water, where they splashed and played. Eve had not seen Jane or Joshua in the veranda dining room at the Plantation great house last night. Maybe they'd had their dinner brought to their cottage. Some guests valued their privacy so much, they never showed their faces in the old Plantation house for meals or drinks.

Eve put her book down and lay back on her own mat, closing her eyes. She tried to think of other things, not see those familiar dark eyes, but all she saw was the face of Parker Adam, the man she had almost married five years ago.

She would never forget his face. After five years it was still etched in her memory.

She sat up, feeling a wave of despair. She didn't want to think about him; it brought back too much pain and regret. Having gathered her things, she came to her feet, and slowly moved toward the path leading up to her cottage which was hidden from view by lush tropical growth.

She glanced up. Perched dramatically on a rocky cliff was the main building, an impressive, elegant plantation house dating back to colonial times when slaves imported from Africa worked the sugarcane fields.

The resort, a hundred and twenty acres of tropical beauty draped around the palm-fringed cove, encompassed the great house, a dramatic swimming pool, tennis courts and fifteen secluded cottages hidden in leafy vegetation, each with its own path down to the beach. It was simply called the Plantation, and reservations were booked one or two years in advance. Famous writers came here to work on their next bestseller, Hollywood movie moguls and European royalty came to escape the limelight and social whirl. The Plantation offered the ultimate in stylish solitude and luxury pampering.

Climbing slightly, the path to Eve's cottage was lined by purple allemanda and shaped by palms and ginger thomas trees. The little house was made of local stone and had handmade wooden shutters and a thatched roof, blending into the cliff as if it was part of it, part of the natural surroundings.

One side of the airy living room was left open *cabana*-style—no glass, no windows, leading out onto a terrace fringed by scarlet hibiscus. The view of the palm-shaded beach and the crystalline blue-green waters was breathtaking.

This was her own hidden sanctuary, where she had lived now for over a year, despite all her father's efforts to persuade her to give up this nonsense and come back to Philadelphia.

Eventually she would go back home, but not yet. For now she was happy here on the island working with the children in the orphanage. She felt needed and loved. It gave her great satisfaction to know she was doing something worthwhile. It wasn't a feeling she'd ever experienced before.

Only suddenly now she felt her quiet existence invaded by a fearful premonition. She saw again the boy's face, the serious eyes, the shape of his head, his determined little chin. She pressed her eyes shut, trying to obliterate the image.

What if Parker was here, at the Plantation?

She moved into the garden bathroom filled with large ferns and potted plants and turned on the shower. She could check at the desk, of course, but she never showed much interest in the goings-on at the resort and she didn't want to attract anyone's attention. The desk was always attended, so she couldn't sneak past to have a look at the guest list.

She could call from her room. She could ask to speak to Mr. Adams and the receptionist would either tell her there was no guest by that name, or he'd simply connect her and she could hang up. She let the water run through her hair and lathered it with shampoo. No—the switchboard would show them it was her calling, and besides, the receptionist would recognize her voice.

She wondered why she was suddenly so paranoid about anyone knowing she was putting a call through to Mr. Parker Adams, venture capitalist from Philadelphia. Nobody would care.

She got out of the shower and dried off with one of the soft, pale aquamarine towels. She stood in front of the mirror, naked, wondering what Parker would think of her now, with her scarred and crippled leg. For the rest she was still the same, tall and slim with full round breasts, the same thick mass of auburn hair and luminous green eyes. Maybe not the same, exactly. She looked older and wiser, and perhaps some of the shine in her eyes was no longer there. If he saw her now, after five years, what would he think?

She turned away abruptly. This was insane! She didn't even know he was actually here.

She dressed in wide-legged trousers of flowered island cotton and a white shirt, getting ready to go to St. Mary's Orphanage. Driving her yellow Mini-Moke, she went up the winding road, leading through the Plantation grounds, turning right onto Old Sugar Mill Road which circled the island.

She liked her little Mini-Moke. It had no roof and no windows and looked like a toy car. With the automatic transmission put in especially for her, she had no trouble driving it.

The narrow road led through fields of sugarcane with the mountains looming beyond, covered with dark green rain forest. Every curve offered another vista of the luminescent Caribbean waters and serene, empty beaches. Eve passed through Ginger Bay, a small fishing village of pastel-colored houses, waving at Father Matthias, who was just coming out of the ramshackle little wooden church. "ARK OF LOVE CATHOLIC CHURCH," the painted wooden sign said. Flower petals and rice lay strewn in front of the old doors, reminders of yesterday's wedding.

Five years ago Eve had been preparing for her own wedding. A big wedding in a big beautiful church in Philadelphia with stained glass windows, an antique altar table and massive silver candlesticks. A sanctuary awash in white and pink roses, spreading their fragrance all through the building...

She could see it now as if it really had happened, this wedding that never had. So long had she planned and dreamed and organized that the fairy-tale fantasy of it all had taken on a life of its own and had become reality in her mind. She could still see in her mind the silk wedding gown with its pearls and delicate embroidery, the masses of roses for the church, the enormous layered wedding cake...

In the end it really had proved to be nothing but illusion, because in the end the wedding had never happened. Eve bit her lip, hard.

The road through the village was narrow and bumpy. In front of the local store Emmaline, in her flowered dress and straw hat, was sitting amid her baskets of pineapple and tomatoes and papayas. The store was painted pale violet and had bright turquoise wooden shutters. An old-fashioned Guinness advertisement sign with a corner missing hung on the wall. Eve called out a greeting, and Emmaline smiled and waved back.

St. Mary's Orphanage was at the edge of the village in an old restored sugar mill. When Eve had first arrived on the island for a couple of weeks' vacation several years ago, the place had been a ruin, and the dire conditions under which the two local nuns cared for ten children had appalled her.

A joint venture between her father and the island government had changed the ruins into a roomy, cheerful building that could house up to a dozen abandoned children. Right now it was home to eight.

Smiling faces and happy greetings welcomed her as she walked through the door. Little Sarah wrapped her thin brown arms around Eve's legs. Sister Bernadette, holding a baby in her arms, was smiling ear to ear.

"Miss Eve! Jacob is trying to crawl!"

Eve took the baby from her, lifting him up above her. "Is this true?" she asked, gently shaking him. His plump brown face broke out in a wide smile and he gurgled delightedly. Eve put him down on the carpeted floor. "Okay, show off your stuff, sir."

He gurgled some more and turned over on his back. Eve lay down beside him, leaning on her elbow. "I'm seriously disappointed," she said sternly. The other children laughed. "Come on," she admonished, "on your knees, everybody! Show Jacob how it's done."

They all crawled around the room, giggling, while she joked and cajoled. It was a game, but a serious game none the less. She watched Timothy who seemed to have made some progress in the crawling department, though she could see by his face that he wasn't enjoying himself. Winston, who was five, was dragging his puny legs, using his arms for leverage. Eve patted his bottom. "On your knees, mister!"

Every day she would come and give physical therapy to the children who needed it, trying not only to improve the physical functioning of their bodies, but to give them confidence and pride in themselves. Usually she would start off with a little group play, then give individual attention to the children who needed it.

After she had finished working and exercising with the children, she read them a story. Her work finished, she could have gone home, but she seldom did. The children loved being read to, and the sessions always ended up with a lot of fantasizing and laughter and play-acting. After lunch she would spend some time with the older children, teaching them how to read and write.

She had just finished the story when she noticed Fiona Keating's small frame standing in the door, clutching a large cardboard box. "Their weekly vitamins," she said, her blue eyes smiling. "Sister Angelica is getting the rest."

"Cinnamon Bay Estates," the box read in blue and red letters. "St. Barlow, West Indies." A few green palm trees completed the design.

Fiona was Canadian. She'd settled on St. Barlow after her marriage to David Keating, whose family, descendants of English settlers, owned one of the few large estates still left on the island. Instead of sugarcane, they now grew tropical fruit and spices for export. Twice a week Fiona dropped off some of the estate's produce—mangoes, passionfruit, pineapples, oranges, bananas, as well as vegetables from her own kitchen garden.

Fiona was back a moment later. She wore a trim denim skirt and a crisp pink and white blouse. Sarah ran over and hugged her legs. Sarah always hugged everybody's legs. Fiona bent down, put her arm around the thin shoulders and kissed her cheek. Sarah smiled; she had the most beautiful smile.

Sarah was four and didn't speak a word. She had been born deaf and was in desperate need of special education, something not available on the small island.

Sister Bernadette came into the room, saying she had some coffee for them on the terrace and that she was ready to take the children outside to play. She smiled shyly, looking small in her short white habit and short cap. She was a local girl from one of the neighboring islands. Sister Angelica had grown up on St. Barlow. Both had taken their vows in a small convent on Jamaica.

"Thank you," said Eve. "Just what we need."

The terrace was shaded by a big mango tree and vines climbed along the railing in a tangle of leaves and orange blossoms. Beyond lay the playground with its wooden structures, built by local carpenters according to a very creative American design.

Fiona ran a hand through her long black hair and sighed. "This is lovely. I had to get out of the house—the kids were driving me crazy!" Fiona and David were parents to a brood of three, a boy and two girls. "I can't wait till they're back in school!"

Fiona had an interesting face, her bright blue eyes a contrast to her black hair, which she usually kept in a long French braid, but was loose now.

Eve poured them each a cup of coffee. "I wonder if you'd do me a favor," she said carefully.

Fiona stretched out her legs, crossing them at the ankles. "Of course, any time."

"You're going to think I'm crazy, but...but I'm wondering if there's someone at the Plantation...a man I'm not sure I want to run into."

Fiona raised perfectly arched brows. "Why didn't you check the guest list?"

"I don't want anybody to know." Eve grimaced. "So I'm paranoid." She bit her lip. "Would you call the Plantation from here and ask to speak to Mr. Parker Adams? If he isn't a guest they'll tell you, and if he is, just hang up when they connect you."

Fiona stirred sugar into her coffee. "Eve, this is really juvenile!"

"I don't care. Do it, please."

"Why don't you do it yourself?"

"They'll recognize my voice. I don't want anybody to wonder why I want to know."

Fiona gave her a curious look. "Who is this man?"

"Someone I used to know."

Fiona smiled. "An old flame?"

An old flame. Oh, God!

"Sort of," said Eve, trying to sound casual. She wondered what Parker would think if he heard himself referred to as an old flame. She gave a nervous little laugh and her cup rattled against the saucer as she set it down. Fiona looked at her oddly.

"I'm sorry," she said. "I'm not being very discreet, am I?"

"It's all right."

They drank their coffee and watched the children.

"It's just..." Fiona began after a pause. "I've often wondered why you're here on the island. You're beautiful, talented, well connected, not to speak of rich. I wonder what brought you here, if you're hiding, doing penance."

Eve looked at Fiona, wide eyed, then she laughed. "Oh, Fiona, you've got some imagination! I didn't come here to hide. And I'm not doing penance for anything. Why can't I live on the island without there being some mysterious reason? *You* live here too."

Fiona grimaced. "I married the wrong man."

"The wrong man?" David was a wonderful man, funny, charming. Fiona was crazy about him, or at least that was what Eve had always thought. "What's wrong with David?"

Fiona laughed. "He was born on St. Barlow and he's shackled to this green rock by this estate that's been in the family for generations."

"You mean to say if you had the choice you wouldn't be here?"

Fiona shrugged philosophically. "Who knows where I'd be? It's a big world out there." She finished her coffee and put her cup on the table. "So I'll call your mystery man. What did you say his name was?"

"Parker Adams."

Fiona nodded and came to her feet, straightening her skirt.

"Fiona..." Eve hesitated. "Five years ago...we were going to get married and..." She stopped. She could not get the words out.

"He dropped you?"

Eve shook her head. "I..." She closed her eyes briefly. "I practically left him at the altar."

"Eve!"

"Four days before the wedding."

Fiona stared at her, face incredulous. "What did he do?"

Of course Fiona assumed Parker had been the guilty party. He must have done something heinous for her, wonderful Eve, to have dropped him like that. But it had not been Parker who'd done the wrong thing.

"He didn't do anything wrong—I did. Please, don't mention it to anybody."

"Of course not." Fiona gave her a searching look, but refrained from further questions. "I'll be right back," she said, and went inside to make the phone call.

It only took a minute or two before she was back, but it seemed like eternity to Eve.

Fiona sat down again, and poured herself another cup of coffee.

''He's there,'' she said.

Eve drove back to the Plantation, her head dizzy with thoughts and memories.

He was here—the man she would have married in the big Philadelphia church with hundreds of guests present.

Just outside the village she braked for a goat that had wandered onto the road, only barely missing him. She pulled off the road and stopped in the shade of an enormous breadfruit tree. Her heart hammering, she rested her head on the steering wheel.

Parker. She had loved him, yes, but not enough. Her love had been selfish and immature. Maybe by definition that was not love at all.

Why then did it still hurt so much to think of him even after almost five years? Why then did she feel such shame when she remembered his ashen face when she'd given him her ultimatum?

She had no answer. She sighed and lifted her face. Father Matthias stood by the car. He was short and bald, and he looked at her with worry in his dark eyes.

''Are you all right, Miss Eve?'' he asked with concern.

Eve had not noticed him coming down the road. She forced a smile. Father Matthias was a good man, well liked in the village. He visited the orphanage regularly to spend time with the children, and he always had a kind word for her.

''Yes, I am, thank you.'' The lie of the century, Eve thought wryly.

Father Matthias gave her a searching look. He was not convinced, she could tell. ''If there's anything I can do for you,'' he said gently, ''please let me know.''

"Thank you, Father," she said, touched by his concern.

She continued down the narrow road. The closer she came to the Plantation, the more her nerves began to jump. She didn't know what to do.

She would have to avoid him. She wasn't ready to run into Parker Adams just yet. She was never, ever going to be ready to run into Parker Adams.

Only it was unavoidable that she should.

The cottage was tidied up when she arrived, with clean towels in the bathroom, a basket of fresh fruit in the kitchenette and a new arrangement of flowers on the glass-topped rattan coffee table. Next to the flowers was a message from Nick, phoned in from one of the neighboring islands. He was planning to be in St. Barlow on Tuesday for a routine visit of the clinic and the orphanage and was looking forward to his usual reward.

She smiled as she crumpled the piece of paper and tossed it in the wastebasket. Nick Warner was an itinerant pediatrician with a mop of flaming red hair and a full, equally red beard. He did not walk the halls of a big hospital doing his rounds, but rather sailed his rounds among the smaller islands that were too poor to be able to afford properly equipped and fully staffed hospitals. He visited small island clinics, consulting with local doctors about special problems. He had done this now for two years, and it was the strangest thing Eve had ever heard of. She'd met him at a party once in Grenada and, hearing his tale, had immediately grasped the opportunity.

If he was interested in special problems, she had some for him. Could she possibly persuade him to include St. Barlow on his "rounds' and visit the orphanage?

"What's in it for me?" he'd asked.

"Not a cent," she'd said.

He nodded. "I didn't think so."

"So you're in it for the money?" she asked.

"That, or coconuts."

Eve laughed. "I see. Maybe we can strike a deal, then. How about dinner at the Plantation, drinks, the works, every time you come?"

His blue eyes widened. "The Plantation?" he queried. The Plantation was well-known and everybody in the islands had heard of the luxury resort.

She nodded. "The one and only."

"That costs a fortune!"

"Not for me it doesn't."

Nick gave her a narrow-eyed look. "Who are you?"

Eve grinned at him. "A charity case. I eat free, and so do my guests."

He sighed. "Boy, do I feel sorry for you!"

She waved her hand in dismissal. "No need—my father owns the place."

He whistled, duly impressed. "So, what's your connection with the orphanage?"

"I'm a physiotherapist," Eve told him. "I work with the children there."

"For money?"

She laughed. "For hugs and kisses."

Nick nodded gravely. "Much better than money."

"I'm glad you agree. So you'll come?"

For almost a year now he'd come every few weeks, visiting the tiny mission hospital in the small capital of Port Royal as well as St. Mary's Orphanage. Afterward they would always go back to the Plantation to have a swim, then watch the sunset over a drink. Later they would have dinner on the large wraparound veranda of the great house: the price for his services.

Eve smiled, wandered into the kitchenette and took a banana from the basket of fruit on the counter. She liked Nick. He liked her. She frowned, feeling a touch of unease. Maybe he did a little more than like her. She sighed, throwing the banana peel away in the bin. Why was it so hard to feel anything more than friendship for a man? In years now she'd not had any deeper feelings for a man.

Love. She felt her heart contract. The only man she had ever truly loved was Parker Adams. Parker Adams, with his serious smile, his solemn eyes. No man seemed able to touch her the way he had, make her feel the way he had.

She closed her eyes and gave a moan of despair. She was thinking of him again. She didn't want to think of him. For years now she'd tried to rid herself of her feelings and memories. She'd thought she'd been able to do it. But it had all come back to her when she'd seen the little boy, the boy with his solemn eyes and serious smile.

And now Parker was here.

She took a deep breath. Well, somehow she would have to deal with it. Tonight she was going to forget it all. Tonight she was going to Daniella's party and have fun.

It was early still. She lay in the hammock, reading, until it was time to shower and dress. She wanted to wear something cheerful, she decided as she looked over her clothes in the big closet. Her party dresses were all long, no minis. She found a flirty yellow dress with a fitted, strapless bodice, drop waist and a swirly silk chiffon layered skirt. She'd bought it in Rome last year when she'd spent some time with her friend Sophie and they'd been in a rather exuberant, frivolous mood.

She smiled at herself in the mirror. The right clothes could definitely cheer you up. She swept one side of her hair up with a comb and attached a few frangipani flowers. They looked pale and delicate against the chestnut colour of her hair. The tan of her skin made her eyes look light. Parker had liked her green eyes. Green crystals, he had once called them in a rare poetic moment.

Forget Parker! She was going to go to a party. She was going to have fun. She was *not* going to think of him all night.

It was not a long drive to the Penbrooke villa, which was situated on a rocky hill overlooking a small cove and the sea beyond. Eve parked the car in the parking area and walked up to the wooden stairs leading up to the large veranda where she heard the voices and laughter of the other guests.

A man was lounging at the bottom of the stairs, smoking a cigarette and watching her approach.

"Do you need some help with the stairs?" he asked easily.

She smiled. "No, thank you, I'll manage. My leg doesn't like to go to parties, but I drag it along anyway."

He laughed. "I'm Andrew Benedict." He dropped the cigarette butt, extinguished it with his foot and extended his hand.

"Ah, the famous Andrew! Daniella told me about you. She used to work in your gallery in Washington, D.C., right?"

"Right, before she got married and took off for Africa. And you are...?"

"Eve Ashwell. I'm her friend."

He nodded. "Well, Eve, let's join the party. I've finished my filthy cigarette and I think they'll allow me back."

It was a large party. Fiona and David were there too. Daniella looked wonderful. She wore a long colorful gown made of some exotic African print material. A wide band of thick embroidery edged the neckline and the wide sleeves. It wasn't the sort of thing you'd think of small, blond Daniella wearing, but she pulled it off.

Daniella seemed happy and relaxed. Marriage seemed
to suit her. She was on a month of home leave from
Ghana in Africa where she lived with Marc, her engineer
husband. The villa belonged to Marc's father, Hayden
Penbrooke, who was in conversation with an American
professor of economics who claimed all the island's
economic problems could be solved by manufacturing
coconut fiber doormats.

Eve sipped some rum punch, entertaining Andrew with
some island jokes, while he reciprocated with the latest
jewels from Washington. She felt herself begin to bubble.
She enjoyed parties. She enjoyed people. Once she'd
done a lot of partying, but that had been years ago. Life
on the island was quiet and uneventful and sometimes,
when the solitude became too much, she would hop on
a "puddle-jumper" and fly to Trinidad and visit friends.
On Trinidad something was always going on.

She hadn't been back to Philadelphia now since
Christmas seven months ago. Sometimes she longed for
the big city ambience, the lights and glamour, the plays
and parties, but not very often. She was busy now with
other things.

So much had changed in the last five years.

She listened to the talk—local politics, the plans for
building a vocational school, the mango harvest, the new
contract signed for the export of star apples to the United
States. The American professor droned on about his
doormats.

Eve moved to the veranda, lifting her long skirt a little
so she wouldn't trip over the hem with her clumsy foot.
She was tired of standing and looked around for a chair.
Andrew waved her over, gesturing to the empty seat
beside him.

"How's the leg holding out?" he queried.

"It's sulking, but I'm tough." She liked his attitude. At least he wasn't trying to pretend he hadn't noticed she had a limp.

He smiled. "I'll bet!" He gave her an admiring look. "How about another drink? Punch?"

"Thanks, yes." She nibbled on a plantain chip while he went over to the small table and poured them each a drink. He sat down again and proceeded to tell her about Daniella's new exhibition coming up at the Benedict Gallery, showing her latest African paintings.

Eve didn't know what suddenly made her feel an odd stirring. She grew very still, feeling something indefinable in the air around her, a sense of breathless expectation. She felt a tingling awareness of another presence, of eyes watching her with great intensity.

She jerked her head up, and her breath caught in her throat.

A man was standing just feet away from her, staring at her.

Her heart began to hammer wildly. Even in the shadowed darkness of the night with only flickering candles on the small tables, she could tell who it was. She knew his shape, the contours of his body.

Parker.

CHAPTER TWO

EVE had not been prepared for this. Away from the Plantation she had felt safe. Now Parker was here, and she couldn't breathe. She felt all the color draining from her face, all strength fading away. Her heart thumped wildly against her ribs.

She had to get away. She felt like a trapped animal and flight was the only thing on her mind. Yet she couldn't move; her body seemed frozen to the chair.

"Hello, Eve." His voice was cool and composed, but held an undertone of surprise. Apparently finding her here on this tiny island had not been on his list of expectations either. He could not have known her father owned the Plantation, but that was quite possible, of course.

"Hello, Parker," she answered, hoping her voice didn't wobble. He loomed over her, tall and broad-shouldered, and she felt small and insecure as she sat there in the chair with him looking down at her. Never before had she felt so unnerved by a man, perhaps because she had never known a man better than she'd known Parker. And no man had known her better than Parker had.

He looked just as she remembered him: imposing and very much in control of himself. On first meeting, people judged him cold and aloof and shied away from him. Not Eve. Eve had considered him a challenge. She'd wanted to break through that cool barrier and find what hid underneath. She'd wanted to see the coolness melt away. She'd wanted to see him laugh.

Eve Ashwell wasn't intimidated easily. Growing up wealthy and supremely confident, she'd been around many people of power and influence and she wasn't easily impressed.

But Parker had impressed her, although at first she hadn't been able to say why. There was something different about him, something that went beyond the handsome face and the imposing stance. Later she had recognized it as character and substance. Parker was a man of strong convictions and integrity, a man who stood by what he believed in and did not compromise his principles. He commanded respect from his business partners and people he dealt with in his venture capital investment company.

It had taken a long time and had been far from easy, but Eve had eventually managed to find the man behind the cool, aloof manner, and she had fallen in love with total abandon.

Most men she found boring. They were too intimidated by her—she was too beautiful, too rich, too sophisticated and too self-confident. Parker had not been intimidated, not in the least, which of course had been one of the reasons she had been so attracted to him.

Despite the fast hammering of her heart, she willed herself to be calm. She looked into his face, seeing the familiar eyes, steady and serious. He was always so serious. How she had enjoyed making him laugh, taking him out on her crazy excursions, having fun, finding the light side to his character.

"You're much too serious," she remembered saying. "You need to loosen up and have a little fun."

"And you, my girl," he'd said with a smile, "are having too much fun for your own good."

"Why?" she'd asked.

"Life isn't all fun and games. One day you're going to discover that."

He'd been right, so right.

"Are you staying on St. Barlow?" he asked politely now.

Eve nodded. "Daniella is my friend," she said, which wasn't the most logical of answers. "I didn't know she knew you." She looked away, her hands trembling in her lap. His closeness was turning her into a quivering mass of nerves. If she reached out, she could touch him. If she closed her eyes, she could remember how it felt to be held in his arms, to make love with him.

"We just met yesterday," he said. "I saw her paintings at the Plantation and I phoned her to see if we could meet."

The Plantation owned an impressive collection of original West Indian art among which were several of Daniella's paintings, displayed in the reception area of the great house.

"Daniella is a wonderful painter," she said. "She's married to an engineer and they live in Africa. They're here on home leave, although actually they're from Washington, D.C. She used to come here a couple of times a year, and that's how I met her, and..." She rattled on, aware of the nervous tone in her voice, not knowing how to stop herself.

"I like her paintings very much," Parker broke in. "How have you been these last few years, Eve?"

"Oh, fine," she said, waving a casual hand. "How's business?"

"Going well. We moved offices."

"You're still in Philadelphia?"

"Yes."

"So what are you doing here?" She was on automatic pilot, asking the routine questions, fighting to keep her composure.

"I'm investigating the possibility of setting up a data-processing operation here."

"What kind of data? From where?"

"From American companies. Billing, mailing lists, credit card transactions, all sorts of things. We'll use..."

She heard the words as he went on to explain, but the meaning did not sink in. All she was really conscious of was the rich, familiar tone of his voice, a voice she had loved, a voice that had said so many secret, passionate words to her in dark, warm nights of loving.

She picked up her glass and took a sip. It was a mistake. Her hand trembled and she knew he was aware of it.

"It all sounds very interesting," she said. "How long will you be here?"

"I'm writing the entire paper. I'll be here for six, possibly seven weeks."

She didn't know how she was going to live with that. It was a frightening prospect. With an effort she pulled herself together.

"Do you like St. Barlow?" she asked, like a polite stranger.

"What I've seen of it, yes. Very lush, very picturesque."

"Very poor," she added.

There was an infinitesimal pause. "Yes." He was still standing, looming over her. "So what have you been doing in the last few years?"

He'd never believe her in a million years. "Oh, a little of this and a little of that," she said casually.

It was a terrible, strained conversation. Eve didn't understand why Parker even wanted to see her, much less speak to her. Her body was rigid with nerves.

Her eyes caught someone else coming on to the veranda. Aunt Janey, the woman she'd seen on the beach that morning. She looked ravishing, wearing a simple but elegant dress in a lovely shade of blue. It was long and slim-fitting and fabulously feminine without being openly seductive, and Eve couldn't help but admire her taste. Janey's hair gleamed like honey-gold silk in the muted light of the candles. She glided toward them, smiling.

"Parker?" She laid a hand on his arm. The left ring finger had a diamond ring and a wedding band. "When you have a moment there's someone you should meet."

Eve stared at the rings, feeling as if all the life was being sucked out of her. Well, what had she expected? That Parker would have stayed unmarried for the rest of his life because she'd walked out on him four days before their wedding?

No, she had not expected that, yet the proof of it in front of her very eyes was more of a shock than she had expected.

In the last few years she'd tried not to think of him and to some extent she'd managed to ban him from the surface of her consciousness. It had been sheer self-preservation. Yet at odd and unguarded moments he would intrude into her thoughts and questions would haunt her. Did he still think about her? Did he love another woman? Had he married? The questions were painful, but they had not vaccinated her against the pain of reality.

"I'll be with you in a moment," Parker said to Janey. "Let me introduce you."

Janey smiled at Eve as Parker made the introductions, but the smile faded as soon as she heard Eve's name.

"Eve?" She gave Parker a quick, questioning look.

"Eve Ashwell." He did not elaborate; there was no need to.

Eve watched Janey. There was no doubt in her mind that Janey knew very well who she was. An image flashed before her eyes—a picture of the two of them talking about her. She could imagine the things Parker had told

Janey, and at that moment she would have gladly died and disappeared from those knowing eyes. The anguish suddenly overpowered her, a wave of such despair, she knew she would dissolve into tears in another minute.

She had to go, had to leave. She could no longer stay here with Parker and his beautiful wife, a woman who knew the worst about her. But before she could get up out of her chair and somehow manage to squeeze past them, Parker gave her a cool nod.

"Excuse us," he said, resting his hand on Janey's shoulder and leading her away.

"Could I get you another rum punch?" Andrew Benedict asked solicitously. "It looks as if you need one."

"No, no, thank you," said Eve, feeling dazed. She couldn't talk now. She had to be alone. She came to her feet. "Excuse me," she muttered, stumbling past him, her left leg feeling weak and awkward in her haste. She grabbed hold of someone's arm, muttering an excuse, and fled into the house, into the room Daniella used as a temporary studio. She sank down on the floor, hugged her knees to her chest and the tears came unchecked, racking her body.

She wasn't sure how long she'd been there, but eventually she calmed herself. She stared unseeingly at one of Daniella's paintings on the wall, a bright blur of colors and shapes. She felt numb, her body limp from exhaustion. For a long time she just sat there, not moving, not feeling anything.

She jerked out of her stupor when the door opened and Daniella sailed in in her long, colorful gown.

"Eve! What are you doing here? Why are you sitting on the floor?"

"I just had to get away."

"From Parker Adams?"

Eve pushed her hair back from her face, and one of the frangipani blossoms fell in her lap. "How do you know?" she asked.

"He's looking for you. Good heavens, Eve, you've been crying! Will you please tell me what's going on?"

"I don't want to see him."

There was a pause. "I didn't know you knew him. I just met him and his wife yesterday. They seemed to be interesting people. His wife is a sculptor, and we sat and talked for the longest time..."

"Oh, shut up, Daniella!" Tears flooded Eve's eyes again. She scrambled to her feet, grabbing the wall for support.

Daniella frowned, her blue eyes troubled. "I'm sorry, I didn't mean to upset you. What did he do to you, Eve?"

She'd never told Daniella about Parker. She'd never told anybody. It was a shameful secret she couldn't bear to bring out into the light. She couldn't bear to think about the person she had once been, the selfish, spoiled-rotten little rich girl. How Parker could have ever loved her was a mystery she would never understand.

"Eve?" Daniella was waiting.

Eve swallowed. "He didn't do anything to me. I did something very stupid a long time ago and...well, it all came back to me and I lost it. I'm all right now, really. I just had to be alone for a while. I'd rather not see Parker just now." She wiped her face. "I think I'll go home."

Daniella gave her a worried look. "You want Marc to drive you back?"

Eve laughed. It was a little shaky, but real. "No, really, I'm all right. I can manage."

She went into the bathroom and washed her face and hands. No wonder Daniella had been concerned; she looked like a disaster, her eyes puffy and swollen, her face flushed, her mascara all over the place. She repaired the damage as best she could.

She managed to slip out of the house without drawing anyone's attention. She walked carefully down the path toward the small parking area below, hearing the voices and laughter drifting down from the veranda. The breeze felt cool on her heated cheeks and she smelled the sweet fragrance of jasmine in the balmy night air.

She got into the car and sat still, staring out over the sea, seeing small lights dance on the water. Fishing boats, probably. The sky was clear, with thousands of stars and a thin sliver of a moon. Music from the house drifted down into the darkness and she heard the high laughter of a woman. She felt alone, more alone than she had felt for a long time.

The sound of footsteps made her look away. A dark shape was coming toward the parked cars. Maybe another early leaver. She put the key in the ignition, ready to switch on the engine.

"Eve?"

Her hand stilled on the key, her heart turning over at the sound of the voice. Helpless anger flooded to the surface. She'd tried to avoid him, and here he was anyway.

"How did you know I was here?" Her voice was husky with anger.

"I asked—I looked all over for you. Daniella said you'd left, but one of the servants said your car was still in the parking area."

"What do you want?"

He shrugged. "I thought after all these years it wouldn't hurt to do a little catching up."

It wouldn't hurt? Maybe not for him. After all, he had a wife and a son and was doing well. Maybe this was his revenge—showing her she hadn't destroyed him, showing he was happy.

Well, she thought wildly, I don't care. I've made a life of my own, not one I'd ever imagined, but I'm happy. He was not going to make her feel bad. He wasn't going to put her on the defensive.

The problem was, he already had. She felt guilty. She felt like a moral midget. She felt angry with herself for having these feelings. She'd left it all behind, closed the door on that terrible chapter in her life. Only here was Parker, opening the door again, and it was all still there and nothing had changed—and all the pain and regret came rushing out again.

Her hands cramped around the steering wheel. "I don't care to do any catching up. It's all a long time ago." She turned the key in the ignition. "I'm going home. Excuse me."

He didn't move away from her car. "The party's just started," he said calmly. He knew she wasn't one to leave parties early, at least she hadn't been. "Why are you leaving so soon?"

"I have a headache," she snapped. It was a poor lie. She seldom had a headache and he knew it. "Now please move over. I'm leaving." She sounded curt and impolite, but she had no strength, no courage for civilities.

"Where are you staying?" he asked.

"I've got my own place," she said, knowing he'd think her father owned a villa somewhere along the coast. Why didn't she just come out and say that her father owned the Plantation and that one of the cottages was hers as long as she wanted to live on the island?

He moved away from the car. "It was quite a surprise to see you here, Eve."

A sleepy little island wasn't the place he'd have expected to find her, of course. She used to go where the action was, the bright lights, the fun, the sports, the music, the people.

"It's a small world," she said lightly. Too small, much too small, she added in thought.

She lay in bed, wide awake, thinking of Parker and Janey, thinking of them being married and sharing a bed. She heard again Joshua's laughter as he played with Janey. They liked each other. The three of them made a family, a perfect family. Once it could all have been hers, if she'd wanted it.

She hadn't.

Not even the breeze rustling the palms outside her window and the soft whispering of the waves onto the sand could soothe her her now.

She was back at the beach the next morning for her customary swim. There was no hiding from reality, and she'd decided not to try. She would have to learn to accept the inevitable. She'd had a couple of lessons in accepting the inevitable in her life, one of them being the fact that her leg would never be the same again, no matter how much money her father had.

She was the very spoiled daughter of a very wealthy man, but this was one situation he had no power over. Sometimes she wondered if it had grieved him more than it had her. He didn't like feeling powerless. He wasn't used to feeling powerless. As he was an international business mogul, his power and influence were widespread. With a flick of his hand he could send phones ringing and wheels turning from New York to Hong Kong within seconds.

He wanted his daughter well, he wanted her leg restored to its former perfection. He didn't want his only child, his beautiful daughter, to go through life with an unattractive limp—crippled, imperfect.

Yet he too had in the end been forced to accept the inevitable.

Up to the time of her accident, Eve had always had everything she wanted in life, except a mother. Her mother had died when she was a year old and she did not remember her. Her father had never remarried, and Eve's grandmother had lived with them and helped raise her. Her father had pampered, indulged and spoiled his beautiful daughter, not only with every material luxury, but also with his time and attention. He never missed a school event, went to every tennis match she played. He loved his little princess and whatever she wanted, she would have.

Absently, Eve took a handful of sand and let it slip away between her fingers. She loved her father, but she often wondered if her life might not have turned out differently if he hadn't spoiled her quite so much.

She wasn't surprised to find Joshua appear at the beach a short while later. He was making quite a statement wearing swimming trunks in orange, green and yellow day-glo colors. She wondered if Parker or Janey had bought these for him or if he'd picked them out himself. No, not Parker at least; quiet, conservative Parker would not have selected something quite so exuberant. Nor would Janey, considering her simple swimsuit and the quietly elegant dress she'd worn the night before.

"I like your shorts," she said, and Joshua grinned a little sheepishly.

"My grandma bought them for me. They're kind of crazy."

"Crazy is good," she said, thinking she might just like his grandmother. "Sometimes, anyway."

"I don't know," he said doubtfully, and her heart contracted. He was Parker's son all right—serious, conservative, uncomfortable in his day-glo shorts. She felt the sudden urge to put her arms around him and hug him to her.

"So what are you reading these days," she asked instead, and his serious eyes began to glow with merriment as he told her.

"It's really good, you gotta read it!" He began to elaborate, and Eve listened, amused, as he told her a time-travel story full of magical adventures. As she watched his animated face, she felt her chest grow tighter and tighter. He was wonderful, this son of Parker's, bright and happy and trusting. A wave of aching regret washed over her, regret so deep and painful, it was suddenly hard to breathe.

She'd carried the shame and regret of what she had done with her for a long time now, hidden deep inside. Yet she knew, no matter how hard she tried, she would never be free of it, she would never be able to forgive herself.

It wasn't Janey who came to the beach to go swimming with Joshua, but Parker. He was wearing dark swimming trunks, a large towel flung over his shoulder.

Eve's heart stopped as she saw him approach and she felt the pain of her nails digging into her hands. She relaxed her grip and took a deep breath, trying not to look at him, at the strong, muscular body that even now still seemed so familiar. For a crazy moment she wished it were five years ago and she could run up to him, hug him, put her cheek against his chest and feel the springy hair tickle her face, smell the warm familiar scent of his skin. She wished she could feel again the strength of his arms around her. But this was now, and he was no longer hers. He belonged to another woman.

"That's my dad," Joshua said to her. He waved his hand. "Hey, Dad," he called out, "I'm here!"

"Good morning," Parker said when he reached them. His tone was polite and impersonal and he seemed not surprised to see Eve there. Probably someone at the party last night had enlightened him as to her whereabouts. It might just have come out in conversation, or Daniella might have mentioned it.

"Good morning," she answered. In the daylight she could see he looked older. He was graying at the temples and there were lines etched beside his mouth. There was a slightly cynical look about him, a bitter twist of his mouth she had never noticed before. She looked away, peering out over the dazzling blue-green sea, feeling her chest tighten.

"Such a peaceful place," he said evenly.

"Yes." She was sitting with her arms around her pulled-up legs, and she was aware that he probably wouldn't notice anything wrong with her left leg unless he looked closely. Not that it mattered. She wasn't normally self-conscious about her leg, but it seemed strange to think Parker didn't know. He hadn't seen her walk last night; she'd been sitting both times they'd spoken.

"So your father owns this place," he said casually. "I didn't know he was in the resort business."

"He's not, really. This is just one of his little pet projects for the fun of it."

"Is he here?"

"No. He's in Tokyo." He'd called her two days ago and talked to her for over half an hour. Wherever he was, no matter how busy he was, her father always called every few days, just to hear how she was and to let her know what he was doing.

Joshua plopped himself in the sand at his father's feet. "Dad, where's Aunt Janey?"

"She's not feeling so well this morning. She's still in bed."

Joshua's eyes widened with worry. "Is she sick?"

Parker ruffled his son's hair. "She'll be all right later on. Don't worry."

"Are you coming swiming with me?"

"Yep, for a little while, then I have to get back to work. Okay, let's go, pal, I'll race you!"

Eve wanted to leave, yet she stayed put, watching father and son playing in the sea, finding some perverse satisfaction perhaps in making herself feel miserable. Two other people came onto the beach, giving her a wave of their hands. They were a couple of well-known Hollywood screenwriters who'd come to the island every year for the past three years, taking out reservations on the same cottage each time.

Having finished swimming and playing, Parker and Joshua waded out of the water, but didn't come back to where Eve was sitting. She watched them disappear among the coconut palms, toward the path that led up their cottage. She felt ignored, left out. It was crazy to feel that way, yet she did.

She gathered up her things and made her way back to the cottage to get ready to go to St. Mary's. At the orphanage she never felt ignored. There she felt wanted and needed.

She spent the weekend with Daniella and Marc and their guests on the Penbrooke yacht, sailing, swimming and scuba diving out on the coral reefs. It was a wonderful weekend, easing some of the tensions Eve had felt in the last few days.

On Monday morning she didn't go to the beach, but had a leisurely breakfast on the terrace before going on to St. Mary's. Fiona came over again with fruit and vegetables and they had a cup of coffee while the children played.

"I met Parker Adams at the party on Thursday," Fiona said as she peered at Eve over the rim of her coffee-cup. "He's quite an intimidating sort, isn't he?"

"I suppose so." Eve watched a yellow-breasted banana quit peck at a crumb of ginger cake next to her foot.

"Did you know he was going to be at the party?" asked Fiona.

"No." The bird flew away and Eve looked up. "He's married now. His wife was with him."

Fiona took a sip of her coffee. "I saw her," she said carefully.

Eve forced a smile. "It's so long ago that we knew each other. It doesn't matter any more, really. It was just...strange seeing him after all these years."

"I can imagine." Fiona fumbled around in her handbag. "Look at this." She handed Eve two photos.

Eve stared at them, transfixed. Then she looked up, incredulous. "Is that little Peter?"

"Yes, it is."

"I can't believe it!" The scrawny little baby who only three months ago had lain in his crib at the orphanage, not crawling, not doing much of anything a baby of over a year should be doing, was now filled out, smiling, walking in the picture. No hollow eyes, no spindly legs. Bright eyes, sturdy legs, happy with the world.

"Maybe they'll want another one next year," Eve said hopefully.

Fiona smiled. "You think we'll have one for them?" It wasn't a serious question. There were always children in need of a home, even on this small island where family ties were strong. The children no one knew what to do with ended up in the orphanage—sick, handicapped children. It was Fiona who had in the last year managed to get five of them adopted, working with an adoption agency in Canada and the local Ministry of Education and Child Welfare, which consisted of Mr. Darnell Robertson and his secretary. Darnell Robertson was also the Minister of Cultural Affairs and Sports, and the owner of the only bookstore on the island.

"I think I've got a place for Sarah," Fiona said on a low note, "but don't say anything yet."

"Really?" Eve let out a sigh of relief. "Oh, I hope it works out! She needs schooling desperately."

Eve's friends often wondered how she managed to do what she was doing, working in the orphanage with these poor disabled children. It was so depressing—the handicaps, the poverty. How could she stand it? Why didn't she come home to Philadelphia? Why didn't she join them for Carnival in Rio? Why didn't she come along to Marbella in Spain for the summer? They called her crazy, held bets on how long she would continue with her "pet project" until she gave it up. She'd passed the three-month bet, the six-month bet, the one-year bet. That was how far they'd gone, and she was still here. They had given up on her. The accident that had damaged her leg must have damaged her brain as well.

Eve knew she could not do this without Fiona's help and the hope she offered the children by finding homes for them. In spite of everything, St. Mary's was a happy place.

Sister Angelica emerged from the house, and Eve called her over. She handed her Peter's pictures, and Sister Angelica's small dark face lit up with joyful surprise. "Peter!" she whispered. She looked up, eyes shining. "May I show them to Sister Bernadette?"

Fiona smiled. "They're yours. Hang them up somewhere."

Sister Angelica hurried off, habit flying, straight into the arms of Father Matthias, almost knocking him over.

It was just after four when Eve came back from the orphanage that afternoon. She parked the car in the shade behind the Plantation great house and climbed out. She heard the low sound of voices coming from the cobblestoned courtyard where afternoon tea was served every day at four according to island tradition, a legacy of British colonial times.

Although the island was an independent nation, albeit a tiny one, reminders of its turbulent colonial past were everywhere, left by Danish, Spanish, Dutch and English conquerors. Port Royal was a jumble of ramshackle Victorian gingerbread, Moorish arches and French provincial architecture. Sturdy, thick-walled Danish warehouses lined the waterfront. A crumbling Spanish fort languished on the north coast.

Eve heard the sound of a child's voice as she rounded the corner of the great house, recognizing it immediately. Further along the path Joshua was approaching her, accompanied by Parker, Janey and the grandparents. There was no way to avoid them now, so she kept on walking, wishing she could put a little dignity in her movements, if not grace. Unfortunately, gliding regally along the garden path was not within the realm of possibility if you had a crippled leg. She held her head high, looking right at the people approaching her. She wasn't sure what she would read on Parker's face when he noticed her ungainly walk, but she didn't care.

"Hi," said Joshua when they were close. "We're going to have tea." He wrinkled his nose. "But I can have Coke." He wore longish white shorts and a neat blue polo shirt—very proper. No neon colors now.

"Hello, Joshua." She smiled at the rest of them. "Good afternoon."

They returned her greeting politely. Janey glanced away when Eve's eyes met hers. Parker's face was devoid of all expression, but then he was a master of control. Then again, maybe he wasn't controlling anything. Why should he care that she had a bad limp? Why should he care about what happened to her at all? She was nothing to him now but a memory, and not a very good one at that.

It was a demoralizing thought. Eve smiled bravely and moved past them. Ahead of her on the path a peacock strutted along in leisurely fashion. There were several on the plantation grounds, some sort of living decoration to beautify the already exotic surroundings.

Back in the cottage she took a shower. She smelled of baby milk. Little Rosie had spat up on her in rather copious amounts. Rosie had been found early one morning just over a month ago at the back door of the orphanage, lovingly dressed in a frilly little dress and wrapped in a threadbare towel. It was suspected that she'd come from one of the other islands, brought in on a fishing boat and dropped off during the night.

Rosie was a beautiful, healthy baby, and the tragedy of her abandonment would never be known. Fortunately it would not be difficult to find a home for her. It would be the paperwork that would take the time.

Eve dressed in a comfortable pair of shorts and a loose blouse and went back to the sitting room. She turned on the overhead fan, picked up the phone and ordered tea, complete with scones and jam and cream. She was going to skip dinner tonight; she wasn't up to seeing Parker and his family on the veranda.

She sat down at the small desk with the laptop computer and began to work. A couple more days and she'd have the article finished. She'd written several now for various publications about the orphanage and her work with the children. It was satisfying to see her work in print and to get favorable replies from readers. She enjoyed the discipline of writing, and it was something useful to do with her time. It pleased her to have discovered another small talent she might never have found if her life had not made such a drastic change after the accident. When some doors closed, others opened. It was true, wasn't it? It had certainly been true for her, although walking through other open doors sometimes cost a lot of effort.

She heard footsteps outside and looked up from the keyboard, expecting the waiter with the tea, but found Parker instead. Her heart made a crazy leap and she stared at him for a moment, not saying anything.

"May I come in?"

No, she wanted to say. Just leave me alone! Instead, she waved her hand in invitation, wondering what had brought him to her cottage. She felt distinctly nervous, to say the least, but was determined not to let it show. She saved her work with a quick stroke.

Parker advanced into the room. "Am I disturbing you?"

"I'll finish later." Her voice was steady, businesslike, which pleased her.

He stood casually in the middle of the room, hands in the pockets of his white cotton trousers. Eve watched him glance around, taking in the surroundings, the desk with the small laptop computer, the photo of her mother, the stacks of books and knickknacks around the room.

"Why are you here?" she asked.

His gaze settled on her face. "What's the matter with your leg?" he demanded, ignoring her question.

"Nothing. It just doesn't perform as well as it used to."

"Why? What happened?" His voice was short, curt, as if he was a lawyer cross-examining a witness.

"I was in a car accident." She felt no compulsion to elaborate.

"When did that happen?"

"About three months after..." She swallowed the last of the sentence. "November five years ago."

"Three months after you canceled the wedding," he conjectured.

Eve looked straight at him, heart hammering. "Right. And I wasn't the one driving, if that's what you're thinking." He'd never liked her driving style, which was quick and somewhat abrupt. He himself drove very smoothly and with great precision.

His face was expressionless. "That's not what I was thinking."

She had no intention of asking him what he was thinking.

"It couldn't have been easy for you," he commented.

"Oh, I managed," she said lightly, seeing with relief the waiter appear in the doorway. He wore white trousers and a floral shirt that served as the Plantation uniform.

"Just put it down there," she said, indicating the coffee table. "Thanks, Erasmus."

Erasmus looked at the tray and frowned. "There's only one cup, Miss Eve. Shall I bring another one?"

"No, thank you. I have cups in the kitchen."

Erasmus retreated. Eve got up from the desk chair and moved to the couch.

Parker sat down in a chair, uninvited. The rattan creaked under his weight. "You're not here on vacation, are you?" he asked.

She shook her head. "No. I live here. I imagine it was easy to find out about me at the party, wasn't it?" she asked, hoping for a note of disdain in her voice. It came out sounding defensive.

"I didn't go around asking questions about you, if that's what you mean."

Of course not. Not his style. Eve picked up the teapot. "Would you like a cup of tea?" she asked politely.

"No, thank you, I had enough." He watched her as she poured some for herself. "You used not to drink tea," he commented.

She shrugged. "Five years is a long time. There are a lot of things I do now which I didn't before—and vice versa."

"Such as what?"

"Use your imagination." She waved her hand at the computer. "For one thing, I used not to write articles, and I do now." She tapped her left leg. "Dancing and skiing I had to give up." She straightened, challenging him with her eyes. "So why are you here? To tell me you're sorry about my leg? Well, there's no need—I'm fine, thank you."

She didn't want him here, she knew that. There was nothing to be gained by it. The past was the past and she had no need to stir it all up.

His eyes met hers. "Is that why you're in hiding here?" he asked quietly. "Because you're so fine?"

Her body tensed. She didn't know why his question suddenly made her so angry. First Fiona, now Parker!

"Don't you think you're just a little presumptuous, assuming you know why I'm here?" she said coldly. "We haven't seen each other in five years. Who do you think you are, to come in here and tell me I'm hiding? What am I supposed to be hiding from, in your considered opinion?"

He shrugged. "The world. Or at least your world."

"I haven't a clue what you're talking about." Of course she did have a clue. She was well aware what was going on in his mind. She could no longer go dancing and skiing and she was no longer the tall, beautiful girl everyone looked at as she entered a room with her graceful walk and beautiful long legs. Maybe she could not face people's pity. Maybe she was no longer comfortable with the glitz and glamour set of the East Coast. Well, he was wrong.

He gave her a probing look, his dark eyes intent on her face. "This isn't at all like you, Eve," he observed.

She gritted her teeth. "How do you know what's like me? You may not have noticed, but I'm not like me any more. But whatever your fertile imagination has cooked up, rest assured that I'm not a pathetic cripple hiding away from the world.'' She came to her feet, wishing furiously she could at least stand straight, but even that wasn't possible. She glared at him. ''I think you'd better leave.''

Parker made no move to go. ''Is your husband here?'' he asked calmly.

The question took her completely by surprise. She stared at him. ''My husand?'' she echoed.

''Walter Harrington. I thought you married him.''

''Oh.'' She looked away, feeling stupid. Walter Harrington was another mistake in her life, fortunately not one that had caused her much grief. The accident had taken care of Walter fast.

''I was going to, but he changed his mind after I had my accident.''

He frowned. ''Why?''

Eve almost smiled—it was such a true Parker question. Loyal to the core, he could not conceive why Walter might have dropped her.

''I couldn't go dancing any more,'' she explained.

One dark brow rose in question. ''Dancing?''

She nodded. ''Yes, as in moving your feet to music. I couldn't walk—I had five operations. I sat in a wheelchair for months, had physiotherapy for years. It was all a big bore, you know,'' she said lightly. ''No fun at all, so he left.''

She hadn't loved Walter. She'd met him in Hong Kong soon after she'd canceled the wedding. He'd been fun to be with and they'd enjoyed each other's company. When he'd asked her to marry him, she'd thought, why not? She'd felt oddly unfeeling about the whole thing, as if nothing really mattered any more.

''I see,'' said Parker. ''When the going got tough, he took off.''

Just as I did, Eve thought wildly, feeling the heat of shame flood into her cheeks. She lowered herself down again on the couch, wishing she could sink away into the flowered cushions, be invisible. She'd thought she'd dealt with the past. She'd accepted it and buried it and gone on with her life. Yet here it was, back again: Parker looking at her, the past come back.

It's over, she told herself desperately. You made a mistake, but that was five years ago. Forget it! It's over!

Yet she knew it was not over. It would never be over. How could it be, with Parker sitting across from her reminding her of that awful time in her life?

"That's why you're here, isn't it?" she asked, her voice tight with controlled anger. "To see how I've messed up my life so you can feel smug and satisfied because after all it's what I deserved. That's what you're thinking, isn't it? Well, you can think whatever you want, but keep your assumptions and judgments and thoughts to yourself!" She came to her feet again. "And now get out!"

CHAPTER THREE

HE STAYED where he was, of course—Parker Adams was not a man given to following orders. Eve saw a faint smile tug at the corner of his mouth, and it infuriated her. He might despise her, hate her for what she had done to him—she could accept all that, but ridicule she could not tolerate.

"Did I say something funny?" she asked with icy fury.

"I'm just glad to see you've not lost your spunk and spirit." There was faint amusement in his voice.

"Why would I have lost that?"

Again the arrogant lift of his left eyebrow. "It's rather obvious, I should think."

She willed herself to stay calm. "Because my life's such a disaster? Well, I hate to disappoint you, but it isn't, actually. My accident was almost five years ago, so I've had plenty of time to learn to live with the inevitable. Having a leg like this is a nuisance, but it's not the end of the world."

"You must have thought so in the beginning."

Her eyes challenged him. "Why would I have thought that? Because I was spoiled rotten and not used to making do with second best?"

His mouth quirked. "Exactly."

"Well, you're wrong," she snapped. "As a matter of fact, in the beginning I thought I'd lose my leg altogether, so when they managed to save it after all, I could only feel happy." She leaned against the desk and a book slipped off, fell on the floor and slid along the tiles.

47

Parker bent to retrieve it, his eyes automatically focusing on the title.

"*Sensory Processing in the Child*?" He gave her a puzzled look.

"Physiotherapy," she said curtly.

He frowned. "Why are you reading that?"

"For professional reasons. I'm a physiotherapist."

He stared at her, seemingly lost for words.

"I got kind of involved in my own case," she explained evenly. "I liked the therapists I had and—well, I became interested. It seemed like a good thing to be doing, so... here I am."

"You went back to college?"

Eve nodded. The accident had wreaked havoc with her normal routines and activities—tennis, dancing, skiing, all of them no longer possible. It had left a gaping void, and taking up studying had filled many empty hours. It had given her a new purpose in life, a new determination to make the best of it. The stubborn streak in her character had been put to good use.

Parker moved to put the book back on the desk, standing very close now, so close she wondered if it was intentional. Her mouth went dry. She could smell a faint scent of after-shave, the same he'd used five years ago. She could see the small lines by the corners of his eyes, the tiny scar above his left eyebrow, and her body flooded with sudden warmth and her heart beat in a fast, frantic rhythm. There were golden lights in his brown eyes and she tore her gaze away, focusing instead on the lock of black hair falling over his forehead. Her hands tingled, as if urged by some mysterious force to reach out and touch his face, his hair, the small scar on his forehead. She clenched them into fists.

"You're full of surprises, aren't you?" he said quietly, and her gaze lowered to meet his. His eyes held hers, looking into their depths for a long, silent moment. "But then you always were," he added on a low note. Turning abruptly, he strode out onto the shaded terrace and disappeared down the path.

He was gone—left in his own good time, not because she'd told him to.

Eve began to tremble all over. She stumbled over to the couch and dropped herself down, suddenly limp with exhaustion as if she'd labored at some impossible task too long and too hard. She picked up her teacup with shaking hands. "Damn you," she muttered. "Damn you!"

She wasn't sure if she meant him or herself.

The next day was Tuesday, and Nick Warner arrived at the orphanage just before lunchtime, transported by Mom's Happy Taxi. Mom had picked him up at the small mission hospital in Port Royal where he'd spent the morning consulting with the local doctors. As always, he had sailed into port on his yacht the evening before and tied up in the marina for the night.

"Dr. Nick! Dr. Nick!" the children chanted. They were always happy to see him, and he entertained them with his antics as they all shared a simple lunch of conch chowder. The nuns too were glad to see him, their faces smiling, eager to do his bidding. He always brought small treats for everybody, and by their reactions of gratitude one would think he was Santa Claus handing out expensive gifts. After lunch he examined the children and discussed their needs with the nuns and Eve. As usual, old Dr. Kimmel made a visit to confer with Nick as well.

After teatime, and more fun and games, Eve and Nick left to go back to the Plantation for a swim in the pool and a leisurely drink before dinner. She always enjoyed his visits and the stories he told of his wanderings around the islands. He was easygoing and entertaining, but despite his casual attitude he took his work seriously.

But this time she wasn't looking forward to dinner as she usually did. Most likely Parker and his family would be there, and she would just as soon avoid being close to them if she could. Yet she had no choice. She couldn't very well cheat Nick out of his luscious dinner, or ask him to go somewhere else. There was nowhere else on the island, not if you wanted five-star *haute cuisine*. The Sugar Bay Hotel in Port Royal served good, hearty island food and for the rest the island sported a number of small eateries serving standard goat stew, fried fish and conch fritters.

They were all there, of course, Parker and Janey and Joshua and the grandparents, all happily eating their first course, talking in animated tones, smiling.

As the *maître d'* showed Eve and Nick to a table, Parker looked up from his plate, meeting her eyes. Her heart gave a nervous little leap and she felt warm under his regard. His eyes glanced over her, taking in her long black floral dress with its swirly skirt and fitted bodice with narrow straps. He would like the dress, she knew; he had never liked the blousy styles that hid the shape of breasts and waists. His gaze moved on to settle on Nick, who seemed oblivious to the scrutiny.

They were seated at a small table two places down from Parker's. It was one of the better tables, right at the veranda railing, catching the warm, fragrant sea breeze and giving a magnificent view of the moon-silvered sea and gardens.

She studied the menu, which she already knew by heart, pretending Parker wasn't there, just two tables down. All she needed to do was look slightly to her left and she would see him. Maybe she should change places with Nick, but the idea of knowing Parker was invisibly behind her was even more uncomfortable. She said nothing.

"Let's have a look," said Nick, his voice eager. "I do so look forward to these little dinners."

Eve laughed. There was no such thing as a little dinner when it came to Nick's eating habits, and she was always amazed at the amount of food he managed to consume.

"I'll start with an artichoke heart stuffed with lobster," he decided. "How about you?"

"I'll pass on the first course," said Eve.

"Spoilsport! I'll feel lonely eating by myself."

"No, you won't. I'll have another glass of wine and watch you." She would try very hard to watch him, and keep her eyes from wandering to Parker's table.

The large wraparound veranda was a lovely place to be. The tables had crisp tablecloths and gleaming silverware. Exquisite Limoges china dishes, crystal wine glasses, fresh flowers and a pink candle in a glass globe were arranged in a beautiful setting.

"Well, let's see. What shall I have?" Nick frowned in concentration. "Pineapple duckling? Snapper Caribe? Poached parrot fish? Smoked flying fish? Ostrich breast?" He sighed. "Decisions, decisions."

Eve was unable to enjoy her dinner with Nick; the uneasy awareness of Parker's presence all but destroyed her appetite. Her neck felt stiff from trying not to turn her head sideways to the left. It was pathetic. It was stupid. So what if her gaze wandered over the rest of the tables? So what if she happened to look in his direction? She turned her head casually to the left. There he was, looking at her, his eyes dark and intense, his face inscrutable in the dim light of the candle. Across the shadowed space between the tables, she could feel the vibrations between them—intangible and almost frightening in their intensity.

She looked away, feeling tense with nerves. Why was he looking at her like that? Why should he care that she was sitting here with Nick?

Although Nick was giving a lot of attention to his broiled turtle steak, his observant eyes missed nothing. She should have known; he was trained to see everything. "What's bothering you, Eve?" he asked.

"Nothing," she lied. "What makes you think something's wrong?" She looked down at the broiled yellowtail on her plate and carefully cut a piece and brought it to her mouth.

"You seem absentminded, and very nervous."

She forced a smile. "I'm sorry—I am a little preoccupied. I'll try and do better."

She didn't do any better. Not as they finished the main course and not as they ate their dessert of mango mousse. Every time she looked up she saw Parker in the periphery of her vision, felt the tension emanating from him. She was aware of the laughter coming from the others at his table as they lingered over their dinner. They all seemed to get along very well.

Halfway through her mango mousse, she put her spoon down. She couldn't swallow another bite.

Nick stroked his beard, giving her a searching look. "Would you rather leave?"

Eve shook her head, feeling guilty. "No, let's have some coffee." Surely Parker and Co. would be leaving soon. They'd been eating before the two of them had even arrived.

"Sure? You don't have to be polite for my sake, you know."

"I know." She smiled at him. He was nice. He deserved better. He had come out here especially for the kids and the least she could do was give him her attention while they had dinner together.

They didn't linger after the coffee. Parker and his family were still there. Nick led her off the veranda, his arm lightly around her shoulders. Parker's eyes burned on her back. They moved out into the shadowed garden, but instead of going on to the parking area for her Moke, Nick made her sit down on a bench.

"Why don't you tell me what's been bothering you?" he asked. "Maybe I can help."

Eve shrugged. "I'm just not feeling very good about myself, that's all."

"Don't we all, at times?"

She smiled in the dark. "Why wouldn't you feel good about yourself? You're a wonderful person, Nick. Think of what you're doing, working in all these small clinics and hospitals. The kids love you. They're always happy to see you."

He laughed, a warm, amused sound. "I can say the same about you, can't I? You don't have to do what you're doing. You're not even getting paid. You could be back in the States living the easy life. Instead, you came here, bugged your father and the Government to get the building restored, get play and exercise equipment, and God knows what else. You're there almost every day, working with those little kids while you could be shopping in Rome or Rio." He took her hand. "You're a generous, loving, unselfish person, and I'd really like to know why you feel bad about yourself."

"You don't know me," she said huskily.

"Ah," he said lightly. "It's all just a cover. In reality you're a mean-spirited witch, or a Russian spy." He squeezed her hand. "Who cares? I like you anyway."

She laughed.

"What's on your mind?"

Eve bit her lip. "Have you ever done something that was really wrong? Something you regret, but that you can't ever make right again?"

"Yes," he said, serious now. "Most people do, Eve. It's called life."

She looked away, staring off into the night, into the shadowed greenery of the gardens. Strangely, his words were no comfort.

"Maybe it helps to talk about it," he said quietly.

She shook her head and swallowed. "I don't think I can." Extracting her hand from his, she came slowly to her feet. "I'd better drive you back."

They found her little Mini-Moke and she drove him back to the small marina in Port Royal. At first light in the morning he would sail away to another tiny island.

"See you," he said, giving her a quick hug. "Hang on in there, kiddo!"

The next morning Eve went to the orphanage early to pick up Timothy and Winston and bring them back to the Plantation pool for some water exercises. The two boys were elated. They were four and five and had lived such an isolated life that even a ride in her little car was a treat.

The pool was big and beautiful, shaped to fit its wild, rocky surroundings. With its crystalline blue-green water it resembled a natural mountain pool crafted by nature itself. Fringed by palms, large-leafed plants and blooming ginger lilies, it was an idyllic place. Small groupings of tables and chairs under thatched shades were tucked discreetly into leafy corners of the lush greenery. As usual only a few people were swimming. The Hollywood couple were there, exercising their slim, sleek bodies. They smiled and waved at her.

She had only been working with the boys a few minutes when she noticed Parker approach, striding up to the deep end and diving into the water with clean, smooth movements of his brown, muscled body. Her heart seemed to turn over in her chest. He hadn't noticed her, and she pretended not to be aware of him as she continued working with the boys. She wondered if Joshua was at the beach with Janey.

Timothy and Winston loved the water and they loved the games Eve had them play. But today they seemed quite rumbunctious and difficult to keep under control. It was no surprise that at one point Winston's wild and flailing arm hit Timothy in the face. Winston's laughing face sobered instantly.

"I'm sorry, Miss Eve, I didn't mean it." It was an accident, and Winston's thin arm couldn't have packed much of a punch, but Timothy none the less broke into tears.

She heaved him out of the water and put him on her lap.

"I'll never walk by myself, Miss Eve," he whimpered.

So it wasn't just his face that was the problem. Her heart ached for him. How well she remembered all her own exercises, the frustration, the fear that she would never, never walk again.

"Oh, but you will!" she said with conviction. "If you keep trying, your leg will get stronger and stronger and you won't need your crutch any more. Promise."

She glanced over at Winston, sitting on the smooth stone steps.

"Winston, splash the water with your legs. Lift your legs one at a time, as high as you can, and keep splashing the water. See how hard you can do it."

He gave her a wide grin, no longer penitent, and tried moving his puny little legs. He had the most engaging smile, with the devil gleaming in his dark eyes.

Timothy was still crying and she was speaking to him quietly when a shadow fell over them.

"Is there a problem? Can I help?" Parker stood dripping water, looming over them.

Eve's heart lurched at the sight of him. "I can manage, thank you."

"Where are their parents?" he asked.

She stiffened. He probably wondered why she was here with two little black boys, why they were seemingly alone.

"They're with me," she said, hoping Timothy hadn't heard what Parker had said. "We're having a water therapy session."

"I see." He looked at her leg, stretched out in all its glaring imperfection on the lounger. She resisted the urge to grab her towel and cover it up. She didn't do it for anyone and she wasn't going to do it for him. Her leg was her leg and that was the way it was.

Timothy lifted his head to look at Parker. He wiped his eyes. Eve gave him a tissue from her bag and told him to blow his nose. "We'll go back in the water and play a little bit more, okay? Then we'll have some juice and a snack." She helped him into the water again, aware of Parker watching her. Her simple black swimsuit hid nothing, and it annoyed her that she felt self-conscious under his regard.

She straightened to face him. "They're from St. Mary's Orphanage," she said on a low note. "I work there—I take some of the kids to the pool here for therapy. But do me a favor and don't say anything about parents, please. They're rather lacking in them over there and I only know about physical therapy, not psychotherapy."

"Sorry," he said. "I assumed the parents were guests here and they left the kids to their own devices. I didn't mean to interfere." His tone was even.

"He's crying because he got hit and he's discouraged," she explained.

His eyes were dark and unreadable. "Is that what you've been doing here for the last year? Working at an orphanage?"

Eve raked her hand through her wet hair and nodded. "Yes." She moved back to the edge of the pool. "Excuse me, please."

She got back into the water, seeing Parker lower himself on the lounger, watching her. She gritted her teeth. Well, he wasn't going to make her nervous. Let him watch.

But he did make her uncomfortable, and she noticed that in the days that followed he seemed to be watching her a lot. Was it just coincidence that she saw him everywhere? At the beach, on the breakfast terrace, in the great house lobby? Maybe it was just her imagination. Sometimes Janey was with him, sometimes not. Janey was always coolly polite and beautifully composed. Every time Eve ran into Parker, he would stop and say something, ask a question, make a comment. The situation was getting on her nerves. She wished Parker would leave her alone.

After a few days she realized that Joshua didn't speak to her at the beach any more. He would play with his ball away from her, waiting for Janey or Parker to come and go swimming with him.

One morning she called his name and waved him over. He came willingly enough, but she sensed a certain reticence.

"How's everything?" she asked. "Are you enjoying yourself?"

He stood by her side, looking uncomfortable. "I'm fine, thank you," he said politely.

"Read any good books lately?"

He nodded, but did not elaborate.

"I liked talking to you in the morning," said Eve. "What's going on?"

Joshua glanced away, his face flushed. "My dad says I shouldn't disturb you."

She felt a stirring of uneasy suspicion. "Why is that?"

"He says people come here to have privacy. They don't want to be bothered." He shuffled the sand with his foot.

"Well, you don't bother me, Joshua. You can talk to me any time."

"Okay." His eyes met hers, his gaze serious. "If you're sure I'm not disturbing you."

"I'm sure. I'll tell your dad, okay?"

He smiled. "Okay."

Janey was coming onto the beach, and he turned and raced off to go swimming with her. Eve watched him go, his voice echoing in her mind. *He says I shouldn't disturb you.* The irony did not escape her. It wasn't Joshua who disturbed her. It was Parker himself. And now Parker didn't want her talking to his son. What did he think she was doing to him? She felt humiliated and furiously angry.

She was tired of the way he was watching her, tired of the way he made her feel. She was *not* going to let him intimidate her, humiliate her. She'd have a talk with him, give him a piece of her mind.

She went back to her cottage, showered and dressed. Joshua's words echoed in her head and her anger grew as the minutes passed.

She found Parker in his cottage, working at the computer on his desk. Like her own, the front of the room was open, catching the cooling tradewinds. A breakfast tray from the Plantation kitchen was on the coffee table with a pot of coffee and a basket of sweet rolls, untouched.

He seemed unaware of her presence. She watched him for a moment before she gently tapped the little bell hanging from the roof overhang. At the sound of it he lifted his head.

"Eve," he said, cocking one eyebrow in mild surprise.

She took a steadying breath. "I'd like to talk to you."

"Come in. Sit down." He waved at the sitting area, the rattan chairs and couch with comfortable cushions upholstered in bright island prints. He looked at his watch and she gritted her teeth.

"I won't take much of your time," she said tightly. She advanced into the room but didn't sit down. Parker pushed his chair away from the desk and stood up. He was barefoot and wore khaki shorts and a blue polo shirt.

"What can I do for you?" he asked.

Eve clenched her hands into fists. "You told Joshua to stay away from me." Her voice shook. "Why?" She knew why, but she wanted to hear him say it.

Dark eyebrows rose. "Why? So he wouldn't disturb you. I've told him in general to leave people alone."

"And me in particular!"

"Why would I do that?" His voice was calm.

"You tell me!"

He put his hands in his pockets. "I don't understand why you're so upset, Eve. I just assumed you wouldn't be interested in him."

She felt the color drain from her face. She hated him for saying what he said, for making her feel small and worthless. She didn't want to feel like this; she'd left all that behind. This was now, and she was not the person she had once been.

"You don't know me," she said, her voice shaking. "Not any more. I like talking to your son. If I don't want to be bothered I'm quite capable of letting him know all by myself." Anger gave her strength. "Are you worried I'll be a bad influence on him?"

He made an impatient gesture. "For God's sake, Eve, calm down! You're overreacting." He moved closer, taking her elbow. "Sit down."

His touch was like an electric shock and she yanked herself free. "Stop patronizing me! If I want to sit down, I'll sit down!" She heard her own voice, recognizing to her horror that she sounded exactly the way she didn't want to sound—like a willful child. Why was it so hard to keep herself under control with him? She felt as if she was going completely to pieces, as if her emotions were running away with her, rendering her common sense powerless. How could this be? Normally she felt quite capable and self-confident, in charge of herself and her emotions. Yet ever since Parker had appeared on the island she'd felt herself regressing, felt long-buried emotions coming back to her. She didn't want to feel the shame and regret every time she saw him. She didn't want to be reminded of her own weaknesses and imperfections.

And that was what he was doing to her, merely by his presence.

He shrugged at her outburst. "Suit yourself." He sauntered over to the table and lifted up the coffeepot. "Would you like a cup of coffee?" he asked calmly.

With an effort Eve composed herself. "No, thank you."

She watched him as he poured himself a cup. "Does Joshua know about me?" she asked. It was a terrifying thought.

"Why would he know about you?"

"Because you might have told him! Because Janey might have told him."

He took a drink of his coffee, his eyes meeting hers over the rim of his cup. "Would it matter if he knew?"

She felt her throat close. "Yes." It was a strangled sound. She felt tears burn behind her eyes, and turned wildly, reaching for the door for support, then felt his hand on her shoulder, felt his touch like a pain.

"He doesn't know, Eve. I see no good reason why he should."

And some very good reasons why he shouldn't. His child's mind would probably assume he had been the cause of what had happened to his father and he'd be riddled with guilt.

She took a deep breath, moved away from his touch, out onto the terrace. Parker did not try to detain her.

Janey no longer came to the beach in the mornings. It was always Parker. Eve enjoyed talking to Joshua, but even the most innocuous conversations with Parker were a strain for her nervous system. She didn't want him to know how much he disturbed her, and it took all her strength to act normal and calm when they were together.

"How's Janey feeling today?" she asked him one morning on the beach. She hadn't seen Janey for days. "Is she sick?"

"She'll be all right," he said calmly. "She'll feel more comfortable once she's home. She and her parents are leaving on Thursday."

"And Joshua?"

"He'll stay here with me."

It didn't make sense. Nothing made sense. If Janey was leaving because something was wrong with her, shouldn't he be going with her?

"What's wrong with Janey? Why isn't she feeling well?" she asked, feeling a sudden, unaccountable apprehension.

He gave a crooked smile, cocking one eyebrow. "You don't know?"

She sighed impatiently. "Why should I know?"

He shrugged. "I thought it was rather obvious, especially to a woman. She's pregnant."

"Oh." Her hands shook. Oh, no! she thought. Oh, no! She felt as if some giant hand was squeezing her heart. For a moment her breath caught in her throat. She didn't know why the news should shake her so, yet it did. Why hadn't she guessed Janey was pregnant? Maybe subconsciously she'd not wanted to know. She didn't want to have one more piece of evidence of how well Parker's life was going, how happy he was. Not because she didn't want him to be happy; certainly he deserved it. It only went to prove how wrong she had been to let him go. As if she didn't know it already, as if she wouldn't regret it for the rest of her life.

Joshua came running up to them, sending sand flying. "Dad, Eve's taking some of the kids from the orphanage for donkey rides on Friday. She says if it's all right with you I can come too." His eager face looked pleadingly at Parker.

Parker gave Eve a questioning look.

She nodded. "I invited him on the condition that you'd agree. It's at a friend's estate, on the north side of the island. She has a son the same age. He's home from boarding school on Barbados and he's bored stiff."

Parker looked at Joshua's eager face. "You're getting kind of bored, aren't you?"

Joshua nodded guiltily. "Donkey rides sound like fun."

"Actually it's therapy," said Eve.

Parker glanced at her. "Therapy?"

"It's good for increasing equilibrium. It gives mobility to kids who don't have much and gives them a sense of mastery."

Joshua was jumping impatiently up and down in the sand. "Can I, Dad? Please?"

Parker gave her a searching look. "If Joshua comes along, won't he be in your way?"

"I wouldn't have invited him if I thought that. I know there isn't much to do here for kids. I thought he might enjoy seeing the estate."

Parker nodded. "All right, then. Thank you."

Joshua gave a shout of excitement and leaped in the air. Parker watched him wryly. "You'd think he was deprived or something," he remarked.

*   *   *

Coming home from work that afternoon, Eve found a letter from Sophie, her best friend from her college days. She sat back on the couch with a smile and opened it. Life was glorious, Sophie wrote. J.J. was the perfect husband, the baby was beginning to crawl, Rome was wonderful, the appartment was being redecorated, and she'd bought five Biagiotti cashmere sweaters. Did Eve remember the Laura Biagiotti Boutique on Via Vittoria?

Eve felt a terrible envy as she reread the letter. Five years ago, just before the wedding, their roles had been reversed. You're so lucky, Sophie had said. The perfect man, the perfect wedding. If you ever come across another man like Parker, you'll let me know, won't you?

Sophie had found her man, had a baby, was happy. She even has five Biagiotti sweaters, Eve thought with an attempt at humor. And look at me—alone. I've messed up my life and lost it all. I don't even have a single Biagiotti sweater.

She dropped the letter on the table, impatient with herself. Well, she wasn't going to sit here and feel sorry for herself. The walls seemed to close in on her. She walked out, down the narrow path to the beach, and sat down in the sand, arms around her knees.

She sat there for a long time, watching the sun slowly sinking into the aquamarine waters, making a glorious display of color in the sky.

Such beautiful colors, such peace and quiet. Yet she felt restless and sad inside. She leaned her chin on her knees. It was no use to pretend to herself that Friday was going to be a day like any other day, just another numbered square on the calendar. It was crazy to let it bother her. In the previous few years she'd been quite capable of not thinking about it. It was because of Parker that it had all come back, that she remembered that day again, that she was incapable of letting it pass without feeling anything.

"Eve?"

She jerked her head up, startled at the sound of the voice. Parker was standing by her side and she hadn't heard him coming.

"Sorry, I didn't mean to startle you," he apologized.

Her body went rigid. Something snapped inside her and anger surged through her.

"What the hell are you doing here?" Her voice shook with uncontrolled emotion. "Why can't you just leave me alone? I don't want you here, don't you understand that? Why are you doing this?"

One eyebrow quirked. "Doing what?"

"Searching me out! Talking to me!"

"Am I?"

"Yes, you are, and you know it!"

His eyes looked into hers. Suddenly he looked very tired. He rubbed his neck as he watched across the placid turquoise waters. "I don't know," he said wearily.

Eve came clumsily to her feet. Whenever she was upset or angry, it seemed harder to move, to keep control over her errant leg muscles. The shifting sand didn't help one bit. Parker took her arm to steady her.

"I'm all right!" she snapped, his gesture fueling her anger—anger because her leg wasn't cooperating, anger because he wouldn't leave her alone. "Don't touch me! Leave me alone!" She turned and stormed off, too fast, and the next moment she went sprawling, landing in the sand.

He was with her the moment she lifted her face out of the sand.

"Oh, damn, I'm sorry," he said huskily. "Are you all right?" He lifted her into a sitting position, brushing sand off her cheeks and chin. She slapped his hand away, crying with helpless fury. And then he was kissing her and she was still crying and everything inside her turned liquid. She couldn't think any more.

She clung to him, tears streaming down her face.

CHAPTER FOUR

ONE blinding moment of insanity as she felt his warm mouth on hers...one delirious moment of forgetting as she felt his familiar touch, his hands on her breasts, the hard pressure of his body against hers... Her heart and body remembered, leaping into life as they always had at his touch.

One moment of insanity.

Then reality struck like a sharp-edged sword, shattering the dream. An image flashed through her feverish mind, a face...Janey's face. Janey who was his wife. Janey who carried his child.

She pushed him away from her with a strength she didn't know she possessed, a strength fired by a wave of hate and loathing so strong it frightened her.

"Don't you ever do that again!" she said fiercely, nearly choking on the words. "How dare you? How *dare* you?" She hated him. She hated him for having such a terrible effect on her emotions. She hated herself for having given in to him, if only for a moment. It was wrong. It was despicable.

Even in the dusky light she could see the paleness of his face. "I'm sorry," he said unsteadily. "I don't know what came over me." He reached out his hand to her. "Let me help you up."

"I don't need your help! I don't need your pity! I want nothing from you, nothing! Just get out of my way and leave me alone!"

She lowered her face into her hands. She had to be calm. She had to get herself together so she'd be able to stand up and walk back to her cottage without falling on her face again.

There was nothing but the seductive lapping of the waves, the soft rustling of the wind in the palms. She lifted her face. Parker was still there, looking down at her, naked despair in his eyes.

"Go away," she said, her voice choking.

He stood there, not moving, not helping, and she came slowly to her feet and carefully walked away through the sand, aware of him watching her, hating him.

Eve did not sleep that night. She lay in bed in her thin cotton nightgown and listened to the sounds coming from outside—the tree-frogs, the sea, the wind in the palms. The shutters on the bedroom window were open and she could see a patch of dark sky studded with stars. All she could think of was Parker holding her, Parker kissing her sandy face. All she saw in her mind's eye was Janey, who was pregnant. He had no right, no right. At three she got up and made some tea and sat in the fan-backed chair on the terrace. She sat there sipping cup after cup until the dawn colored the sky and the birds began to sing. Two more days until it was Friday. Tomorrow Janey and her parents would leave.

Somehow she managed to drag herself through the day. Father Matthias came to visit the children, and she was glad to see him. As always, the children climbed on his lap and he told them stories from the Bible, injecting liberal doses of humor without losing the meaning of the stories. Eve liked him and enjoyed his visits. He was always pleased to see her, always making a special point of asking her how she was and if there was anything he could do for her. She had the secret suspicion that Father Matthias thought she was lonely.

Before he left, he took her aside. "Miss Eve, is something wrong?"

"I didn't sleep well. I'm just tired today."

"Will you let me know if there's anything I can do?"

She nodded. "I will."

He patted her hand. "Come to church some time." He smiled, his eyes gleaming with sudden humor. "I know you're not a Catholic, but God will forgive you."

Eve couldn't help but laugh. "Oh, Father!"

"Ah!" he said triumphantly. "A smile! That's what I wanted." He turned and walked off, chuckling.

She went home early from St. Mary's, crashed on the bed and fell asleep almost instantly. It was almost dark when she awoke a few hours later. She called the Plantation kitchen and asked them to send her some coffee. It arrived just as she had dressed after a quick shower that had failed to revive her. She felt groggy, and she sat hunched on the corner of the couch sipping the strong local brew.

"Miss Ashwell?"

Eve looked up, instantly alert when she saw Janey step onto the terrace. She wore white shorts and a blue silk blouse and she looked cool and pretty.

"Yes?" She looked into the deep blue eyes and felt herself tense with trepidation.

"I'd like to talk to you."

Oh, please, Eve thought in despair. I'm not ready for this. "Come in," she said, waving her over.

Janey advanced into the room, but did not sit down. Her blue gaze was fixed on Eve's face. She swallowed visibly, but her eyes didn't look away. "This isn't easy for me, but I felt I had to speak to you." Her voice was quiet and steady.

Eve was not sure what to say. Obviously Janey was here to talk about Parker. Eve sensed she was nervous and trying hard to control herself. She was not going to break down or plead.

"Have a seat," she said, waving at one of the rattan chairs.

"No, thank you."

Eve was not surprised. Janey hadn't come for a social visit with tea and cookies. She was going to have her say and do it standing.

"What is it you want to speak to me about?" she asked, shifting around on the couch and tucking her legs under her.

"I've seen quite a change in Parker these last two weeks," said Janey, diving right in with the courage of the desperate.

"I don't know what you mean."

Janey met her eyes straight on. "I think you do. Ever since he realized you were on the island he's been moody and depressed. He angers easily and seems very preoccupied—it's not hard to guess with what."

Eve tensed. "Are you saying that's because of me?"

"Yes, that's exactly what I'm saying." Janey pushed her hands into the pockets of her shorts. "It was quite a shock for him to see you here. It's not what he'd expected."

"I hadn't expected it either," Eve returned dryly.

"I'm not saying you had. I'm aware that you've lived here on the island for a while."

"About a year now."

"What I wanted to say is...I just don't want..." Janey straightened her shoulders, fixed her eyes determinedly on Eve's face. "He was hurt very badly five years ago and it's taken him a long time to get over it, and now you're here and..."

Eve wondered what it would feel like to be married to a man who had once loved someone else who then appeared on the scene again. She felt sorry for Janey, who seemed so desperate and so proud.

"What is it that you want from me?" she asked at last.

There was a loaded silence. "I want you to leave him alone," Janey said finally, her voice flat.

A humorless laugh escaped Eve. She couldn't help it. She'd said the same thing to Parker last night. Leave me alone.

"It's funny, is it?" said Janey, her voice cold.

Eve shook her head and sighed. "You don't understand."

"I understand all too well!"

Eve stared at her, feeling warmth flood into her cheeks. "Are you insinuating I have designs on him?"

"All I know is what I see, and I don't like what's happening to Parker."

Eve felt anger rise to her throat. Parker was searching *her* out, not the other way around. She'd been trying to stay out of his way. In the mornings she wasn't even going to the beach any more just so she wouldn't have to run into him. "I can't help what's happening to Parker!" she said angrily.

Janey said nothing, the silence eloquent.

So she thinks it's all my doing, Eve thought. She's afraid to leave tomorrow. She thinks once she's gone I'll consider him fair game. "You don't think much of me, do you?" she said.

Janey gave a light shrug. "I only know one side of the story. What I do know is that Parker was devastated. I also know he loves his son." She met Eve's eyes, not wavering. "Even though I only know a few facts, it's very difficult for me not to be judgmental about you, but I'm trying. The fact is, though, that whatever the circumstances, whatever the reasons, you hurt him badly.

You left him when he needed you most. What I'm re-
questing now is that you leave him his peace of mind
and stay away."

Eve was trembling. "I'm quite aware of what you're
thinking of me, but you may rest assured that I have a
few scruples left, surprising as that may seem to you."
She was aware she sounded sarcastic and defensive, and
it wasn't what she intended. More than anything now
she wanted to display some dignity, but she couldn't help
feel the guilt take over, and whenever that happened her
defenses rallied at full speed.

Janey looked straight at her. "He was quite shocked
to find out about your accident. I'm sure it was dev-
astating for you, but..."

"I don't need Parker's pity, nor anyone else's!" Eve's
voice trembled. "And if you think I'm using my leg to
get Parker's sympathy, you're quite mistaken!" She felt
furious, suddenly. "I'm not after him! I'm quite aware
that I messed up his life once. Don't worry, I have no
intention of doing it again." She took a deep breath.
"However, I do live here. I do eat in the dining room.
I do swim in the pool. I cannot dig a hole in the ground
and hide for the next few weeks. Also, I want you to
understand that I have no control over his moods and
depressions."

Janey's soft features tightened. "I'm not so sure about
that."

Eve clenched her hands into fists. "I don't know what
you're insinuating, but I do have a piece of advice. If
you think I'm a threat, then the best solution is to get
him off the island."

Janey looked at her coolly. "He's working, as you
may know." She gave a humorless little laugh. "To think
he took this job to get a little vacation out of it so he'd
have some time to spend with Joshua. Such irony!

Normally he wouldn't have done this job—one of his junior people would take care of it." She sighed and lifted her hair back from her forehead. "At any rate, he's not going to leave in the middle of it now. He doesn't run away from problems."

No, he wouldn't. How right she was! "I don't mean to be a problem," Eve said, her voice calm now. "If I'm perceived as such, I can't help it."

Janey's eyes met hers. Then, without another word, she turned away, walked out onto the terrace. Eve watched her go. It was hard not to respect that woman. She wished she could dislike her. It would make everything easier.

Thursday passed quietly. Eve took Timothy and Winston swimming in the pool, but Parker did not show himself. She didn't see him for the rest of the day.

Then came Friday. Just another day, Eve told herself, eating a solitary breakfast under the almond tree on the terrace. Today I'm taking the children to Fiona's for donkey rides. Tonight I'm going to the Sugar Bay Hotel for the Foreign Aid cocktail party, see if I can't get something out of somebody. Friday, August the seventeenth. Just another day.

The kids loved to ride the donkeys. Joshua immediately hit it off with Kevin, Fiona's son. Despite the general success of the day and the joy of the children, which usually was quite enough to make her feel happy, she felt depressed.

After she came home that afternoon, she found Nick on her veranda, asleep in her hammock. She had not expected him, but felt oddly comforted seeing him. She gave the hammock a push and his eyes flew open. His face broke out in a grin.

She laughed. "Surprise, surprise! What brings you here?"

"I was in the neighborhood."

She gave the hammock another push. "Oh, I see."

She didn't. Nick had never just dropped by. With all the miles of Caribbean between the islands, dropping by was not a casual accomplishment.

"I had some time off, so I thought I'd check up on you," he explained. "Are you feeling better?"

"I'm not sick."

"I didn't say you were."

"I'm fine." She sat down on the fan-backed chair.

"How about dinner at my place?" he asked. "I'll cook—I have some fresh lobsters."

Eve hesitated. "I'd like to, but I'm going to a party tonight and I really should go. Would you like to come with me?"

Nick swung his legs over the side of the hammock. "What kind of party?"

"The American Foreign Aid people are throwing it. All the island hotshots will be there, and I need to find out if Darnell Robertson has made his formal request for a Peace Corps volunteer to help out at St. Mary's. You can help me. Actually it will be great if you'd come with me. It will give me credibility."

He sighed. "I feel used."

She patted his shoulder. "There you go. Now you know the ugly truth. I'm a selfish person, using people for my own purposes."

"I don't like to be used."

"Come on, Doc, rise above your own petty feelings. Let me use you."

He laughed. "You do have a way about you!"

Eve dressed in a cool silk dress, in a blue-green leafy design, a lovely little thing she'd bought in Singapore over a year ago when she'd gone with her father on a business trip. It had an Oriental look about it, simple and chic and not too revealing, just what she needed for tonight.

The Sugar Bay Hotel in Port Royal was an old colonial building of baby-blue stucco and white-trimmed windows. It was a simple place with more charm than chic with its high-ceilinged rooms, big fans and old, dark furniture. Faded red carpeting hailed back to more glamorous times, as did the crystal chandeliers and antique mirror in the entryway. The walls were festooned with old prints and paintings depicting charming scenes of smiling slaves in colorful garb laboring away on the sugar plantations, singing and dancing. Eve had grave doubts about the reality of those idyllic scenes on the paintings.

Apart from the Americans, she knew most of the people already present. On a small island everybody knew everybody. Her gaze scanned the room in search of Darnell Robertson, but didn't find him. Rounding a corner into another room, she almost bumped into a flowered chest.

"Fish!" she exclaimed, stepping back. Fish was a giant of a man, a black American from Chicago with a shaved head, an enormous smile and laughing eyes. He wore white chino pants and a loose floral shirt, looking distinctly more comfortable than some of the other guests attempting to look important in their dark suits and ties. Their faces were shining in the tropical temperature, somewhat destroying the effect.

Eve smiled up at him. "What are you doing here?"

He laughed. "I flew some of these jokers over here earlier and I'm flying them to Antigua in the morning. They put me up here for the night and invited me to come to this shindig."

Fish and a West Indian friend from Trinidad had started their own small "puddle-jumper" service, flying private clients between islands in their small twin-engine planes. Eve liked Fish. He'd flown her around several times and the Plantation guests used his services as well. He liked telling stories and had his own unique way of looking at the world.

He glanced around and sighed. "Man, oh, man, these are very boring people!"

Eve laughed. "Government, politicians, business people."

He gave her a look of desperation. "I'm not going to last. Would you consider blowing this joint? We'll find us a good rum bar and have some fun."

"I'd like to, but I'm here on business."

He shook his head in reproach. "You too? You disappoint me, woman."

Nick arrived with two drinks. The two men started a conversation and Eve took off to mingle.

She was good at affairs like this. She knew just how to mingle, just how to talk to people. More importantly, she knew how to make people listen to her and give her what she wanted. Within a short time she had been introduced to some of the visiting Americans, people who had contacts that might prove to be helpful to her. She had plans for the future and she needed all the influence and help she could gather.

A tiny orphanage in a restored sugar mill on an insignificant little island in the West Indies probably didn't rank high in importance in the cosmic scheme of things. Taking on the cosmic scene was beyond her capabilities. St. Mary's Orphanage was not. She would do whatever it took to get help.

Disengaging herself from a small group of people, she took another glass of wine from the tray of a passing

waiter and searched around for someone else to connect
with.

Connecting with Parker was not on her program, and
when she noticed his broad back as he stood hob-
nobbing with the Minister of Finance, who was also the
Minister of Commerce and Industry, she felt a rush of
irrational anger. What the hell was he doing here? Wasn't
there any place at all she could go without running into
him?

It wasn't really such a coincidence, she knew that. A
gathering of this nature attracted all the people in power,
and with his multimillion-dollar investment project
Parker was undoubtedly an invited guest of major importance. As she herself was not. Actually, she was not
invited at all. But she was the daughter of Randall
Ashwell, owner of the Plantation, and no one was going
to refuse her entry.

Parker turned suddenly, as if he'd felt her gaze on his
back. Their eyes met across the room, and Eve felt a
shock go through her at the look in his eyes. There was
an odd tenseness about him. She doubted if it had anything to do with the meeting he was having with the
Government people at the party. This job was peanuts
compared to his other ventures.

Her legs began to shake. Oh, damn! she thought.
Today, of all days, she had not wanted to see him. It
was hard enough remembering without looking at him
in person. Yet here he was, looking at her, coming
towards her, and she couldn't move. She just stood there,
feeling trapped.

"Hello, Eve."

"Hi." She took a sip from her drink, willing herself
to relax.

"I'm surprised to find you here," he said.

"Why? Don't tell me. It's not like me?"

A faint smile touched the corner of his mouth. "Who's that man I've been seeing you with? Is he with AID?"

"Which one?" she asked.

"The one with the red beard."

"Oh, that's Nick. He's a pediatrician, and he comes and checks up on the children at the orphanage now and then. He's here with me to further the cause of St. Mary's. And you?" she asked politely. "What are your objectives at this illustrious gathering?"

Parker gave his empty glass to a waiter and put his hand in his pocket. "Just testing the general climate for our venture here, and to meet some people I've not yet met."

Such polite conversation! They were doing famously. Eve smiled, searching for a line to facilitate her escape.

"Do you know what day it is?" he asked before she managed it. His eyes held hers.

She felt her heart turn over. There was only one reason for him to ask that question. She shrugged casually. "Friday," she said evenly. Her nails dug into the palms of her hands.

"August the seventeenth." He held her gaze, his eyes dark and intent, and she could not look away. "Our wedding day," he added.

"We didn't have a wedding day."

"No, you're right, we didn't have one." His voice was oddly expressionless.

Eve clenched her hands by her side. "What's your point?" she asked coolly.

"I guess there is no point, apart from the fact that I still remember it after five years."

"What's that supposed to mean?"

"I'm not sure. Except that along with the date, I also remember you." There was no inflection in his voice now and she couldn't make out if he was bitter, angry or simply indifferent.

"I'm sure you do," she said carelessly. "It was going to be rather a big event." It didn't surprise her that he remembered it. What surprised her was that he mentioned it to her. Was he trying to figure out her feelings about it? See if she felt regret or pain? She had no intention of letting him see how she felt. It was no longer any concern of his to know what was in her heart and mind. She steeled herself against the memories. They still held far too much power over her—so much power, in fact, that she was afraid even to think about it with Parker here looking at her. She didn't want to rake up old memories, days of happiness and expectations.

"Why haven't you married yet, Eve?" he asked suddenly.

She gave him a look of surprise. "I didn't want to." She smiled brightly. "Besides, who'd want me? I'm no longer a showpiece, you see. Damaged goods are hard to sell." She had no idea where the words came from, what sort of perverse impulse had taken over.

Parker's eyes narrowed. "That's a very cynical attitude!"

She sighed. "Well, yes, but grounded in reality, wouldn't you say? Ideally, I should be waiting for the man who'll be able to see past the imperfect exterior straight into my beautiful, selfless soul. Problem is, I don't have such a beautiful, selfless soul, do I, Parker? You of all people should know that."

The muscles in his face tightened. By the look in his eyes, she knew she had shocked him. It gave her a perverse sense of triumph. "So, where do I go from here? A damaged body and a black soul don't make a good combination. But I have money. Maybe someone will want me for my money. All hope is not lost." She smiled cheerily.

Why was she putting on this show? Why was she acting as if she had absolutely no sense of her own value? She didn't believe for a minute that her leg would keep a man from loving her. She was no longer the selfish, spoiled-rotten little rich girl, so why was she making herself out to be what she wasn't? Was it some sort of tactic to draw him out and have him tell her what he thought of her? She felt a yearning to have it out in the open, to know what it was he was thinking about her.

"Stop it!" he said, his voice low and rough. He took her arm and propelled her out of the double doors into the shadowed garden.

"What the hell is the matter with you?" he demanded.

"Everything, obviously." Eve looked away, watching the moon peeping through the palm fronds swaying in the breeze. "Why do you care, anyway? Is it fun for you to see me the way I am now? You must be very happy you didn't end up with me as your wife. Don't think I don't understand it, Parker—I do. You're quite right to be happy. I was spoiled, shallow, selfish and stupid. And don't think for a moment that I blame you for feeling the way you do, because I understand that very well too, only have the decency to keep..."

He grabbed her arms hard and his eyes burned into hers. Then his mouth descended on hers in a fierce, tormented kiss that shocked her to the very depths of her soul. There was passion, anger, love, pain in that kiss, all the emotions she was feeling herself, all the emotions that had been tormenting her for the past weeks. They washed over her now and she had no defense. No defense against his powerful hold and the terrible anguish of his kiss.

He tore his face away suddenly, his eyes, dark and fierce, boring into her. "Why do you think I wanted to marry you? Because you were beautiful? Because you had a perfect body with two beautiful long legs? Because you were rich?"

Eve was shaking. She had to get away from him, from the terrifying emotions coursing through her. Her tongue was frozen, tears hot behind her eyes. She wrenched herself free, forcing herself not to run, not to go too fast so she'd end up on her face in the grass.

She searched the crowd inside, finding Nick. She took his arm. "Let's leave," she said, the words squeezing out of her.

Nick stared at her. "Sure." He put an arm around her shoulders and led her out of the room without another word.

"I'll drive," he said, when they got to her car. He took the keys from her fingers and she did not object. She sat next to him, staring out into the dark, until slowly she calmed down.

"Sorry to drag you away," she said. "Were you having a good time?"

"Actually, you rescued me from this terrible bore in plaid trousers who was explaining to me how manufacturing doormats will raise the island to economic glory."

"Oh, no, the magic carpet man!" Despite herself she laughed. "I met him once. I thought he'd be gone by now."

They had arrived at the small marina. The yachts bobbed lightly up and down in the gentle swell of the water. "How about coming aboard and I'll show you my newest toy?" Nick asked as he got out of the car. He looked at her, his eyes smiling, teasing.

"What kind of toy?" she asked quasi-suspiciously.

He laughed. "It's an espresso machine. My sister sent it to me—an attempt at showing me how good life can be if only I'd come back to Minneapolis. So how about a cup?"

"Yes, I'd like that." She had no desire to go home to her empty cottage. She got out of the car, taking the keys from him. Nick took her hand as she maneuvered across the narrow gangplank and stepped onto the deck.

It was a small yacht, meticulously maintained. Eve had been on it several times and once had sailed with him to Grenada when he had invited her for a party. The yacht was his pride and joy as well as his home and vehicle of transportation.

"It's in the galley," he said, preceding her into the small, neat kitchen space. Her gaze swept around, settling on a gleaming black and stainless steel contraption on the counter. "Espresso or cappuccino?" he asked.

"I'll have cappuccino." She watched him fiddle with coffee and water and cups. Hissing noises ensued. A shiny spout foamed up some milk which he poured on top of the espresso.

"*Voilà!*" he said triumphantly. "Easy as pie. Come on, let's go up on the deck."

Under a starry sky they sat and talked, as they always did, about the children, about Nick's career, which was drifting aimlessly. His family were pressuring him to come home to Minneapolis and take over his uncle's lucrative practice before he'd have to sell it to a stranger when he retired.

"Don't do what you don't want to do," Eve told him. "How's that for advice?"

"Maybe good, maybe bad. Can you see me, thirty years from now, gray and decrepit, sailing from island to island, maybe even getting lost, just so I can have money to eat? All I'll own is this boat and my espresso machine." He sighed heavily.

Eve laughed and made an expansive gesture. "But you'll be free, and you'll have the sky and the sea."

"You're downright poetic." Nick put his cup down and took her hand, pulling her up from her chair and into his arms. His mouth brushed over hers briefly. "You'd better go before I get poetic."

She didn't move. His beard tickled her face. Maybe this is what I need, she thought. Nick's arms around me. He's a good man. I like him.

"Eve?" His mouth closed over hers in a more passionate kiss. "You want to stay here with me?" he asked softly.

She wanted to say yes. She wanted to feel loved and wanted. She wanted to rid herself of the lonelieness she had felt for the last few years. A loneliness she'd tried to ignore by studying and working.

She leaned against him, her eyes closed. All she saw was Parker's face. It would not be fair, not to Nick, not to herself.

Parker. Parker who was married and out of reach. Parker who had come back to haunt her. Parker. Pain engulfed her. She moved out of Nick's arms, tears filling her eyes.

"I'm sorry," she said thickly. And then the tears flowed over and a sob escaped her. She began to tremble, and he drew her back into his arms, holding her, steadying her.

"It's all right," he said soothingly. "It's all right."

There was no way to contain the grief. It came pouring out, and she cried until she had no strength left, and all the time Nick was holding her, saying nothing.

When it was over he put her down in a chair and brought them each a glass with some Scotch in it. "Drink this," he ordered. "It'll help."

"I'm sorry," she said miserably. "I didn't mean to do that."

He gave her a crooked smile. "Hey, what are friends for?"

Eve sipped the drink slowly, but it still burned her throat. She never drank liquor straight.

"So tell me," he said casually, "what brought that on? What happened at the party?"

She looked into her glass. "Five years ago today I was going to get married, only it didn't happen." She swallowed at the constriction in her throat. "The man I was going to marry is staying at the Plantation and he was at the party tonight."

Nick whistled softly. "Did he walk out on you?"

She bit her trembling lip and shook her head. Tears were filling her eyes again.

"I walked out on him." Her voice shook. "Four days before the wedding."

"Why?" he asked gently.

"Why?" There was bitterness in her voice. "I called it off because I was selfish and stupid and spoiled. He loved me, I know that. Don't ask me *why* he did, I'll never understand it."

"Start at the beginning," Nick said quietly. "What happened? Why did you call it off?"

Eve closed her eyes, and it all came flooding back, as if it had been waiting to be released—all the details, the awful, self-serving things she had said to Parker, his white face, the whole nightmare of that fateful afternoon when he had come to see her to tell her the news.

He'd come for love and support. She'd given him rejection.

CHAPTER FIVE

FOUR days before the wedding, at five in the afternoon, the wedding gown was delivered to the house. Half an hour later, Eve's friend Sophie waltzed through the big front doors, fresh off the plane from Paris, dressed in a red Chanel mini and three-inch heels. With her straight black hair, dark eyes and fair skin, Sophie was your basic knockout beautiful.

She hugged Eve. "Sorry, sorry, I smell like a plane, but I couldn't wait. I've got to see that dress!"

Eve laughed. "It's good to see you too. And the dress just got here."

Sophie waved her hand impatiently. "Show me, show me! It sounded absolutely *gorgeous* the way you described it!"

They climbed the wide, winding staircase up to the second floor of the large old Philadelphia house where Eve had lived all her life.

"I'm so glad you chose ivory," Sophie said, breathing hard from loping up the stairs. "It's so much better with your coloring than white."

Eve opened the heavy oak door to her room. It was large and bright, with a beautiful antique four-poster bed that had belonged to her grandmother. After the wedding, while Eve and Parker were on their honeymoon in Italy, her father would have it moved to their house, where new silk Pratesi linens were waiting. Eve had loved her grandmother and missed her deeply after she had died a few years ago. Her grandmother had been a true Southern lady, sweet and charming, the daughter of a wealthy New Orleans merchant. The bed had come from there, transported to Philadelphia when she had married Philip Ashwell, Eve's grandfather.

Sophie followed Eve into the room, suddenly silent as her eyes focused on the long, puff-sleeved wedding gown draped on its bust form. The ivory silk satin gleamed richly in the late afternoon light. The dress had a sculpted, off-the-shoulder sweetheart neckline and lavishly hand-beaded Schiffli embroidery on the fitted bodice, along the hem of the full skirt and on the sweeping train.

"Oh, Eve!" Sophie whispered in awe. "It's the most beautiful dress I've ever seen!" She moved over and gently touched one of the pearls on the basque waist. "It's a dream!"

Eve smiled. "I'm glad you like it. I was really upset, you know, when you deserted me at the last moment. I wanted you to help me with the design."

Sophie grimaced. "Paris was a big bore. I'd much rather have been here with you, helping you get ready." She eyed the wedding gown longingly. "Put it on for me, please?"

Eve hesitated, then smiled. "Sure." She slipped out of her white trousers and blouse and with Sophie's help carefully put on the dress. It fitted her to perfection, as it should. It had been designed especially for her at astronomical expense. Her father had been adamant. Only the very best for his only child, his beautiful daughter—a fairy-tale gown for the lovely princess.

Sophie stepped back and surveyed Eve in the dress. "It's perfect! You're so tall and slim, it's absolutely perfect." She sighed with envy. "You're so lucky, Eve. The perfect man, the perfect wedding. If you ever come across another man like Parker, you'll let me know, won't you?"

Eve laughed. "I'll capture him, wrap him up and send him to you by express mail!"

The intercom by the door buzzed. Eve picked up the receiver. "Yes?"

"Eve?" It was Mrs. O'Reilly, the housekeeper. Mr. Adams is here. Shall I send him up?"

"Yes—*no!* My wedding dress! He can't see it!"

Mrs. O'Reilly laughed. "Oh, goodness, no!"

"Tell him I'll be right down." Eve replaced the receiver and looked at Sophie, and they broke out in a silly giggling fit.

"I didn't know he was coming!" said Eve, swallowing her laughter. "I'd better get out of this thing. Help me, please."

A few minutes later, safely clad again in trousers and shirt, she went back down the stairs, followed by Sophie, who was trying to tell her in twenty-five words or less about her boring time in Paris.

"You don't have to leave," Eve said when Sophie headed for the big doors in the marble-floored entry hall. "Why don't you stay for dinner? I haven't seen you for ages and I want to talk."

Sophie shook her head. "I've got to go and shower the plane smells off me. Say hello to Parker. We'll talk later."

Eve hugged her. "I'm glad you're back. Come for lunch tomorrow?"

"Okay, great." Sophie smiled her radiant smile and swung out of the door. "Bye!"

Parker was waiting in the living room. He stood by the large bay windows overlooking the landscaped gardens, his back turned to her. Eve liked his back. She liked the straight line of his shoulders, the shape of his head. She liked everything about him and she loved him madly. She felt a rush of warmth and excitement. In four days he would be her husband.

"Hi," she said, smiling, her voice a little husky. He turned and she went up to him, put her arms around him and kissed him. "What a nice surprise! I thought you had that meeting with those people from Mexico."

"I canceled it."

She stared at him. Parker did not cancel important meetings for nothing. "Why? I thought..."

"Something came up. We need to talk." The tone of his voice set off alarm bells in her head.

"What's the matter?" she asked, all kinds of scenarios running crazily through her head. He'd had second thoughts. The wedding would have to be postponed, canceled. He didn't love her any more. He wanted out. She looked at his unsmiling face, feeling panic soar. It happened, didn't it? Weddings got called off at the last minute. Grooms didn't show up...

"I had some news today," he told her, turning toward the small bar in the corner of the room. "Do you mind if I have a drink?"

She shook her head, watching him as he poured himself a Scotch. She noticed the slight trembling of his hand and fear clutched at her heart. It was not like him to be so shaken.

"What kind of news?" she asked, steeling herself.

He took a swallow of his drink. "I don't know how to tell you this, Eve." There was a look of pleading in his eyes, a look she had never seen before.

She swallowed hard. "Are you telling me you want to call off the wedding?"

He gave her a startled look. "Good God, no, of course not!" He put his glass down on the coffee table and drew her into his arms, holding her so tight, she could barely breathe. "What made you think that? I love you.

I need you." He kissed her almost frantically, and she felt the fear flow out of her.

She drew away. "Please, Parker, tell me what's wrong."

"Nothing is *wrong*. It's just that something has happened and everything has changed now and I didn't know. I never knew." He raked his fingers through his hair, his eyes grave and troubled. She had never seen him so off balance. Parker was always in control.

"What happened?" She couldn't imagine what he was talking about.

He took her hand. "Let's sit down." They sat down on the couch. "I got a letter from a lawyer this afternoon." The words came with difficulty. His hand clasped hers. "He told me I have a son."

She stared into his face, uncomprehending. "You have a what?"

"Pamela and I have a son. I didn't know."

Eve couldn't think. It felt as if someone had lowered a rock on her head and was squeezing the life out of her.

Pamela. She'd heard the name before, of course. Pamela was the woman Parker had been involved with for several years before Eve had met him. She had never met Pamela, and Parker, the soul of discretion, had never divulged the intimate details of his relationship with her. He'd told her the breakup had been amicable and had been a mutual decision.

"He's three years old. The letter was from Pamela's lawyer."

"Nice touch," said Eve, finding her voice along with an explosive rage. "She didn't have the guts to tell you herself? And she had to throw this at you right now that you're getting married? What a low thing to do!"

His face went white. "Eve!"

She jumped up from the couch and stood in front of him, her legs trembling. "So what does she want? Sue you for child support? And why now? Is she trying to get back at you? Does she want you back?"

"Stop it!" He came to his feet and grabbed her shoulders. "Stop it right here!" His grip hurt and his voice was cold and angry.

Tears of anger sprang to her eyes. "I think it's a rotten thing to do!"

"Pamela's dead." The words dropped like rocks in the sudden silence. He released his grip on her. "She died last week."

Her legs shaking, Eve dropped back down on the couch. Her outburst had left her oddly weak.

"She left a will," Parker went on. "The lawyer told me that if I wanted to claim my son, there'd be no problem; the papers are all in order."

Eve swallowed hard. She knew she had to ask. "And if you don't?"

"His maternal grandparents will get custody."

There was a silence. She tried to think, to make sense out of all this. "But you're not forced into anything?"

"No."

"He doesn't even know you. He'd be happier with his grandparents."

The words hung in the silence.

"He's my son," Parker said at last. "I'm his father and he belongs with me."

Parker had a son. Eve visualized him as a father, which wasn't hard at all. He liked children. He wanted children. When she'd dreamed of their future together, she'd seen him with a little boy in her mind's eye. But the boy had been hers and his, not some other woman's child, and the unfairness of it all made her want to scream with frustration.

"You've never even seen him!" she protested.

"That's beside the point, Eve."

"It's crazy! This whole thing is crazy! How come you didn't even know anything about this?"

"I expect she didn't know she was pregnant when we decided to separate. We certainly hadn't planned it."

"So why didn't she tell you later?"

Parker sighed, and he looked very tired. "I've thought about that and I'm quite sure I know why, but it doesn't matter now."

Eve came to her feet again, restless, afraid, angry. "How do you even know he really is your son? Maybe he's someone else's, maybe she decided..."

His face went rigid, his mouth a tight line. "I never had any reason to think she was lying to me or deceiving me. I have no intention of starting now. She deserves my trust and respect, now as always."

"So why didn't you marry this paragon of womanhood?" She was beyond reason now, saying things she shouldn't say, yet she couldn't help herself.

"Eve," he said, his voice deadly calm, "we're not discussing my relationship with Pamela. We're talking about my son."

"So you're accepting this boy as your child sight unseen?"

"Yes."

Just like that. *Yes.* No questions, no doubts.

"I think you're being irrational and irresponsible!" She felt like stamping her foot. "Don't you think..."

"What I think is that I need to know where you stand." His mouth was grim, his features taut.

She stared at him. "You'll want him to live with us?"

"Yes, Eve."

A three-year-old little boy. She'd have to be his mother. There'd be help in the house, of course, but she'd still be the mother, doing mother-things—helping him brush his teeth, playing with him, reading him bedtime stories. She'd have to watch over him, worry about him eating his vegetables . . . Another woman's child. She couldn't face it. It wasn't the way she had planned it to go. It wasn't at all what she wanted. She wanted to be free and enjoy being married for a while. After a few years they'd start a family, that was what they had decided. She wasn't ready to be an instant mother to a strange child, to have him disrupt her plans, her life, her marriage.

"Will you come with me to the lawyers tomorrow?" asked Parker.

Her body grew rigid. "I won't have time. There's too much to do. The flowers, the photographers . . . I . . ."

"All right," he said, interrupting her. His face was a cold mask. He came to his feet.

"If you're only doing all this out of duty, Parker, you're doing nobody any good, least of all that little boy!" she told him.

His eyes held hers. "Duty? Yes, I'm doing my duty, Eve. I've never run away from my responsibilities, even if it was possible. But I'm not claiming him only because he's my responsibility."

"What other reason is there?"

"I want him. He's my son and I want to be his father. I want to give him my love and support and I want to see him grow up to become a good man. That's what I've always intended to give my children. And he is my child."

"But he isn't mine!"

He said nothing, his eyes dark and unreadable.

"I think you're crazy!" she lashed out. "If Pamela wanted you to be a father, she should have told you when she was pregnant, not dump him on you like this!"

"What Pamela should have done or shouldn't have done is irrelevant now. The facts as they stand now are that I have a son and I want him."

"And what I want is irrelevant too, isn't it?" Her tone was caustic. She saw him flinch.

"No, Eve, it is not." He was calm now, so very calm. It made her furious. How could he stand there and say that? How could he say it was important what she wanted, yet make a decision without asking for her opinion? He wasn't forced to take that little boy; there was a perfectly good place for him to go. He couldn't force her to be a mother. He had no right to expect that of her.

He stood, silent and straight, watching her. "Are you with me, Eve?"

"No!" she yelled. "I'm not going to stand for this! This isn't what we'd planned! I'm not ready for this! You have no right to change things on me just like that! I don't want..." Tears flooded her eyes. "You'll have to decide what you want. It's me or him!"

The color drained from his face. "There's no such choice, Eve." His voice was cold now. *"You'll* have to decide if you want me with my son or not at all. That's the only choice there is, and it's yours to make."

She stared at his white, desolate face, her heart racing. "I don't want to be an instant mother. You've got to understand that."

"Sometimes we have to make adjustments."

"Adjustments? Is that what you call it?"

"Life isn't always perfect, Eve, not even for you. No matter how well you plan, no matter how much money or power you have, life still demands adjustments."

"You're right about that!" she snapped, her voice shrill with rage. "The wedding's off!"

* * *

Of course he would come around. The wedding was only days away. Surely he would come to his senses. He loved her. He wanted to marry her.

Eve tried to tell herself this as she lay awake at night, terror in her heart.

But he didn't come back. Not the next day, not the day after that.

"If you don't want to go through with it," her father said, "you don't have to." From her father she always got what she wanted. He didn't care what inconvenience it caused anybody. If she didn't want to have a wedding, then she didn't have to have one.

A few phone calls later, the wedding arrangements were canceled and plane tickets to Hong Kong reserved. She was going to spend some time with friends and drown her sorrows in a whirlwind of parties and shopping sprees.

Staring out over the dark, placid waters of Sugar Bay, Eve told Nick everything, not sparing herself. She had never actually recounted the whole sorry tale to anyone, and she had no idea what his reaction would be.

It was a struggle to get the words out, to tell the ugly truth of her utter selfishness. After all that had happened to her, she could no longer understand how she could have been so shallow and unfeeling.

After she was finished, Nick looked at her silently.

She grimaced. "A real sweetheart, wasn't I? I'll never understand what he saw in me, why he loved me."

"I'm having a very hard time believing all this, Eve."

"Why? You think I'm making this up?"

Nick shook his head. "I just don't recognize you in that story. It's not at all like you."

"It was me all right," Eve assured him.

"What happened?" he asked.

"What happened when?"

"Afterward. You're not that same girl, Eve, no way, no how. What made you change?"

She shrugged and patted her left thigh. "Life taught me a lesson. More than one, actually. After my accident I spent a lot of time in hospital and I had lots of time to think. I came to the realization that perhaps I'd valued the wrong things in life. I met some wonderful people, nurses and physiotherapists, who gave me some insights I'd never had before."

He smiled. "You've got guts, you know, telling me all this."

She bit her lip. "Thanks for listening. I've never told this to anyone."

Nick took her hand and squeezed it. "I hope it helped."

"I think so."

There was a pause. "Do you still love him?"

Eve looked away. "It was all a long time ago. I haven't seen him in five years." She swallowed. "Besides, he's married now."

It was late when she came back to the Plantation. She parked the car and slowly walked along the path to her cottage. She didn't want to go to bed; she didn't feel like sleeping. She considered going to the bar to find some company, but that didn't appeal to her either. Instead, she strolled aimlessly around the grounds, past the other cottages, all secluded and hidden by bushes and trees. Crickets and tree-frogs held their nightly concerts and the warm air carried the scent of night-flowering plants.

Passing Parker's cottage, Eve saw a glimmer of light through the greenery. He must have returned from the party. Joshua wasn't there; Fiona had invited him to stay the weekend at the estate to keep Kevin company. Eve smiled as she remembered Joshua's voice as he'd spoken to his father over the phone.

"You oughta see this place, Dad! It's awesome! They've got donkeys and cows and cinnamon trees. Did you know cinnamon came from trees? It's from the bark! And they've got weird fruit too. It's called star apples, but they're not apples, but..."

Eve realized that she had stopped moving and was staring at the light coming from Parker's cottage.

You know what day it is? he'd asked at the party.

But it was past midnight now, so it was no longer their wedding day. She closed her eyes. It would have been their wedding night.

After the wedding party, a limousine would have taken them to Forester Castle, a secluded, historic inn in the wooded hills of Pennsylvania.

The small, romantic-looking castle had been built with craftsmen and materials imported from Europe, commissioned by a Henry S. Forester for his bride more than two hundred years ago. It looked like something from the Middle Ages with its towers and turrets and thick stone walls covered with ivy.

They would spend their wedding night in the romantic Tower Suite with a view of the wooded hills of which they probably wouldn't see much at all... There would have been roses in the suite, she was sure, and candles and more champagne. If she closed her eyes, she could still see the silk charmeuse nightgown with its antique lace and narrow straps, handmade in France.

The next day her father's company jet would have flown them to Italy for their three-week honeymoon on the island of Capri, which offered romantic solitude as well as unlimited opportunities for water sports and cultural entertainment if they wanted some diversion.

A tree-frog gave a high-pitched squeal and Eve began to walk again, faster now, back to her own cottage. There was no sense in thinking about these things now. It was useless sentimentality. Besides, it wasn't the honeymoon on Capri that was so important, or the wedding night in the tower of a castle. It wasn't the house they would never live in, the house filled with treasures of beautiful furniture, china, silver, crystal and silk Chinese rugs. It was love that would have given her happiness, love that she had squandered carelessly and lost.

Another woman had Parker's love now. Another woman lay in his arms at night. Another woman carried his child...

"Oh, God," she moaned, "stop it, stop it!" She sank down on one of the stone steps carved out in the rocky path and hugged herself hard. "Don't think about it," she said to herself. "Don't think about it."

Even in the warm air, the stone step felt cold. After a while, she got up and slowly climbed the rest of the path to the cottage.

She lay in bed, unable to sleep. Finally, in frustration, she got up, wrapped a silk kimono around her naked body and went outside. She curled up in the fan-backed chair and stared at the stars. A soft breeze blew in from the sea, fanning her warm face.

All she could think of was Parker alone in his cottage, the lights on. What was he doing? What was he thinking?

It wasn't much later that she heard footsteps coming toward her. Her heart began to race. It was well past three in the morning. It was quiet and dark and almost everyone was asleep in bed.

It was no mystery who was coming to see her.

CHAPTER SIX

PARKER emerged from the shadows of the ginger thomas trees. The light from the living room illuminated his big frame as he stepped onto the tiled terrace. He wore shorts and a T-shirt and his hair looked slightly disheveled.

"I thought I might find you here," he said, his voice low, as if afraid he might wake someone.

"It's three in the morning!" Eve said with prissy indignation. "You don't go visiting people at that hour." She sounded like a prudish spinster, but it was the first thing that popped into her head. She wanted him gone. She was not ready to deal with him while she felt so emotional. She didn't want to look at him, at the dark hair falling over his forehead, at the tanned, muscled legs. She didn't want to look at any part of him. He was too familiar, too disturbing standing there in front of her in the warm, velvety darkness of the night.

"I saw your light on." He paused. "Are you alone?"

Alone? Of course she was alone. Then she thought of Nick. Parker had seen them together a couple of times now. If Nick was staying with her for the night, what would she be doing out here on the terrace alone? Well, it wasn't Parker's business one way or the other.

"What are you doing here?" she asked, not answering his question.

"I couldn't sleep." He stared up at the sky. "I was counting stars. I think I got them all, and I was still awake." Surprisingly, his voice held a tone of humor.

"How many?" she asked.

NO RISK, NO OBLIGATION TO BUY ... NOW OR EVER!

CASINO JUBILEE
"Scratch'n Match" Game

Here's how to play:

1. Peel off label from front cover. Place it in space provided at right. With a coin, carefully scratch off the silver box. This makes you eligible to receive two or more free books, and possibly other gifts, depending upon what is revealed beneath the scratch-off area.

2. You'll receive brand-new Harlequin Presents® novels. When you return this card, we'll rush you the books and gifts you qualify for, ABSOLUTELY FREE!

3. If we don't hear from you, every month we'll send you 6 additional novels to read and enjoy months before they are available in bookstores. You can return them and owe nothing, but if you decide to keep them, you'll pay only $2.49* per book, a saving of 40¢ each off the cover price. There is **no** extra charge for postage and handling. There are **no** hidden extras.

4. When you join the Harlequin Reader Service®, you'll get our subscribers-only newsletter, as well as additional free gifts from time to time, just for being a subscriber!

5. You must be completely satisfied. You may cancel at any time simply by sending us a note or a shipping statement marked ''cancel'' or by returning any shipment to us at our cost.

YOURS FREE!

This lovely heart-shaped box is richly detailed with cut-glass decorations, perfect for holding a precious memento or keepsake—and it's yours absolutely free when you accept our no-risk offer.

CASINO JUBILEE
"Scratch'n Match" Game

SCRATCH HERE

PLACE LABEL HERE

CHECK CLAIM CHART BELOW FOR YOUR FREE GIFTS!

YES! I have placed my label from the front cover in the space provided above and scratched off the silver box. Please send me all the gifts for which I qualify. I understand I am under no obligation to purchase any books, as explained on the opposite page.

(U-H-P-08/92) 106 CIH AFN9

Name _____

Address _____ Apt. _____

City _____ State _____ Zip _____

▲ DETACH AND MAIL CARD TODAY! ▲

▼ DETACH AND MAIL CARD TODAY! ▼

BUSINESS REPLY MAIL
FIRST CLASS MAIL   PERMIT NO. 717   BUFFALO, NY

POSTAGE WILL BE PAID BY ADDRESSEE

HARLEQUIN READER SERVICE
3010 WALDEN AVE
PO BOX 1867
BUFFALO NY 14240-9952

NO POSTAGE
NECESSARY
IF MAILED
IN THE
UNITED STATES

"Billions and billions and billions and two thousand, four hundred and fifty-three."

"You got it wrong. Go back and start over." Her voice was calm, but her mind was in turmoil. Please go back, she pleaded silently. I don't want you here.

"I'm sick of stars."

"Go and take a walk on the beach." Just leave me alone!

"I already did. Your Hollywood friends were there, skinny-dipping, so I left."

"At three in the morning? Well, why not!" At least they were having a good time, which was more than she could say for herself.

Parker rubbed his neck. "I thought I was the only one up at that hour." He looked at her. "Why are you up?"

She met his eyes, feeling anger surge through her. Damn you! she thought. Why do you think I'm up? All I can think about is the wedding we didn't have, the wedding night I didn't spend with you.

"I'm sure you know," she said, trying to sound calm. "You've tried hard enough to make me remember. It should have been our fifth anniversary. It would have been our wedding night five years ago." Calmness deserted her and her voice shook. "I'm not going to play games with you, and I won't have you play your cruel little games with me!"

"What games?"

"You hate me. You still hate me for what I did five years ago and now you're exacting your revenge by reminding me, and showing me how well you've adjusted and how wonderful your life is." She took a deep breath. "Don't you think I know what you think of me? Don't you think I've thought the same myself? I don't need you to keep pointing it out to me! I want you to stay out of my way and out of my life! It's five years ago, and I'm not going to go through all this again. You're history! Our relationship is history!''

"It still seems to disturb you quite a bit," Parker said evenly.

"Yes, it does! I hope that gives you satisfaction. I was wrong—I made a mistake. Five years ago I thought the world was mine. Five years ago I was going to be married to...to...to the man I loved. Then everything fell apart." Eve closed her eyes tightly, taking a deep breath. "Because I was selfish and shallow and spoiled. It's not something I'm proud of, it's not something I'll ever forget. But I have to try and live with it. And I was doing pretty well until you..." Her voice broke and she bit her lip. She averted her face.

"Until I showed up on the island," Parker finished for her. He frowned. "It's an amazing coincidence, isn't it?"

"What is?"

"Both of us on the same tiny island."

"Yes." She gave him a suspicious look. "Did you know I was here?"

"No, I didn't. I didn't even know your father owned the Plantation." He shrugged. "Maybe it was fate."

Eve gave a humorless little laugh. "Fate? What do you think fate had in mind? A little joke?"

He gave her a long look, then turned away, saying nothing. She watched his back, the straight line of his shoulders. She wished she didn't feel this terrible need to touch him, feel his warmth. It was crazy, crazy to feel like this. She averted her gaze, looking up at the dark canopy of the almond tree above her head. If he wasn't leaving, she wished he'd sit down. He was too big, too tall, looming over her in the dark.

"Just out of curiosity," he said after a silence, "what did your father say when you told him the wedding was off?"

Eve gave a low laugh. "My father said that if I didn't want to get married, I didn't have to. Then he made two or three phone calls. That took care of the festivities. No sweat." For the people behind the scenes it must have been a nightmare, with hundreds of guests to be called and all the arrangements to be canceled.

"Your father is putty in your hands. Such a strong man, it's amazing," Parker remarked.

"You're stronger than he is."

He turned to face her. "Oh?"

"You weren't putty in my hands."

He gave her an odd look. It almost made her smile.

"You have your principles and you stand by them, and nothing can change your mind. Not even I could." Her voice was even, just reciting the facts. She was not blaming, not accusing. After all, how could she fault a man who stood by what he believed in? He had given her up, the woman he said he loved, the woman he wanted to marry. But she hadn't deserved his love, so he was better off without her anyway.

"Don't think it was easy," he said softly, and there was pain in his voice.

She stared at him, but in the moon-shadowed darkness it was hard to see the expression in his eyes. "You must have hated me," she whispered.

"Yes," he said. He turned away again, shoulders slightly hunched, as if he could not bear to look at her.

Pain wrenched at her heart. Well, what had she expected? He had loved her and she had treated him abominably. She'd thought only of herself.

"I think you'd better go," she said. She couldn't stand this any longer. "You shouldn't be here."

He turned. "Why shouldn't I be here?" He gestured vaguely at the interior of the cottage. "Is the good doctor in?"

Eve gritted her teeth. "No." She wasn't going to play games and pretend she had a man in her bed when she didn't. "You know very well why you shouldn't be here, and I have no intention of spelling it out for you." She looked at him squarely. "I want you to leave me alone, Parker. I mean it! Janey is already suspicious. She came to see me the other day and..."

"Janey came to see you?" Surprise registered in his face, his voice.

"Yes. Janey isn't stupid, Parker," she said mildly. "She has eyes. She can add one and one."

His jaw hardened. "What did she want?"

"What do you *think* she wanted? She's not at all happy to know I'm here, and I can't say I blame her. She told me she wanted me to leave you alone. I'm trying, but you don't make it very easy for me, do you?"

He stood very straight, his eyes furious. "She had no damn right to come here!" He jammed his hands in his shorts pockets. "What else did she say?"

"That I'd hurt you enough. And she had every right to come here and tell me that, even if she was wrong about me forcing my attentions on you. Whatever else she might think of me, I don't go after married men!"

Parker stared at her. "What the hell are you talking about?"

"I'm saying that I want you to stay away from me. We've dug up the past sufficiently. I'm quite sufficiently miserable, if that gives you any satisfaction. The past is over and you've got a new life. You're married, so..."

"Married?" He gave her an incredulous look.

"You forget fast," Eve said caustically. "How convenient! Maybe you're only married when she's around.

I've met other men like you. As soon as your wife leaves and is out of sight, you're single again, with all its freedoms and privileges.''

''What wife?''

She stared at him, feeling anger dissipate and confusion take over. ''I mean Janey. The pregnant one, remember? The one who left on Thursday morning.''

He closed his eyes. ''Janey is not my wife.'' He opened his eyes again and stared at her dumbfounded. ''What in heaven made you think she's my wife?''

''It seemed rather obvious.'' Eve was glad she was sitting. She felt as if she was going to faint. ''Who is she?''

''She's Pamela's sister.''

Pamela. Joshua's mother.

Her hands trembled in her lap. ''I thought you were married. I thought she was Joshua's stepmother.''

''She's his aunt.'' He sighed. ''Her husband had to go on a business trip to Europe and I asked her to come with us for a little while.''

''So the baby...''

''Don't worry,'' he said bitterly, ''that one's not mine.''

Eve felt the blood drain from her face. She got out of the chair and walked into the night, down the path to the beach. She sank down into the sand, rested her arms on her knees and lowered her head. She was shaking all over. Listen to the waves, she told herself. Listen to the wind in the palms. Everything is so peaceful...

''Eve?''

She stiffened. ''Go away!'' she said, her voice muffled. She raised her head. ''I don't need your sarcastic little digs! Get away from me!''

''No.'' Parker was standing in front of her and he pushed her down in the sand. Leaning over her, he held her down, his face very close. ''Five years, and you haven't forgotten. Well, I haven't either! Do you have any idea what it meant for me to lose you, any idea at all?'' His voice was low and furious. ''I thought I'd learned to live with it too, and then I came here and there you were. And I want you just as much as I ever wanted you. I hate you for what you did. I hate your shallow, selfish ways, and all I can think of when I see you is holding you again, laughing again, loving again. I must be some sort of masochist!''

Her heart was pounding with fear. She had never seen him so angry.

''Do you have any idea what I went through while you took yourself off to Hong Kong for a goddamned shopping spree? Here I was with a three-year-old I didn't know. We were sure a great twosome. He'd just lost his mother and I'd just lost the woman I thought would be my wife. If it hadn't been for Janey and her parents I don't know how I could have coped with it. I would lie in bed thinking of you, wanting you, needing you, hating you. Not a pretty emotion, is it? Hate. It's ugly and it eats away at you and...''

''Stop it!'' she cried. ''Stop it, stop it, stop it!'' Tears flooded her eyes. ''Let go of me! Let go of me!'' She struggled, but it was no use. He lowered himself on top of her, holding her down. There was no way to escape.

His arms came around her, his head down against hers, cheeks touching. ''I kept thinking how it would be, the three of us,'' he went on. ''I never thought it would be easy, but I needed your love and understanding. I thought that together we could make it work. But you...you didn't even want to try.''

Eve gave up the struggle and let herself grow limp beneath the pressure of his body on hers. She was crying silently now, not caring any more, just letting the tears flow and flow, coming from some deep well of misery, until finally they stopped coming. She realized Parker was no longer talking. He was still holding her and she felt his body trembling against her. He lifted his head and with a groan covered her mouth with his.

She let it happen. There was no way to stop it, and she could no longer think clearly. She didn't want to think—it was too painful to remember the words he'd said to her.

He pushed her kimono aside, freeing her breasts, kissing them, his mouth hot and eager. She felt desire flood through her blood like warm wine, intoxicating her, making her light-headed. But it wasn't enough, not enough to obliterate what had just happened, to forget the bitter anger of his emotions. She began to struggle.

"Stop it!" she protested. "Stop it, Parker! I don't want to!" She was crying again. "Don't, Parker! Please don't!" She tried to twist away from his searching mouth, his exploring hands. "I don't want to!"

"Yes, you do," he said fiercely. He struggled with the knot in the kimono belt.

"You hate me!" she sobbed. "How can you do this when you hate me?"

His body grew still. He rolled away from her onto his back in the sand, staring up into the sky, at the stars. "I don't hate you," he said huskily. He flung his arm across his face and groaned.

Eve sat up, brushing the sand off her arms and legs, straightening the kimono, shivering. It wasn't cold. It wasn't the sultry night air that made her shiver. "Why, then? For old times' sake?" Her voice was bitter. "For revenge?"

Parker said nothing, but when she came to her feet he reached out and took her hand.

"Don't go." He pulled her back down, and she sat on her knees in front of him. "I want you so," he said huskily. "I've missed you so. I kept dreaming you'd come back some day." He sat up and drew her against him. Her cheek lay against his chest and she could hear the solid beating of his heart.

He had waited for her to come back, but she hadn't. The stubborn streak in her character had made it impossible—that, and the selfish conviction that he had wronged her by choosing his son over her.

"I want you," he said again. "I thought I was over you, but I'm not." His mouth sought hers, feverish, demanding. "Tell me you want me too. Tell me!"

A storm of desire unleashed within her. All the passion of those many years ago blossomed again in the heat of the moment, the sound of his voice. Her mind bloomed with memories of long, warm nights full of love and laughter. Nights full of sweetness, tender touches, loving words murmured in her ear.

His hands were touching her now, his mouth hungrily kissing hers. His warm, strong body made her come alive, and she felt the painful need to have again what she had lost, to be loved again. She wanted the pain gone, the nightmare over.

"I want you too," she whispered, but her voice seemed not her own. Some strange delirium had taken over. She felt him move, then he was standing, stripping off his clothes, tossing them carelessly in the sand. Her mouth went dry as she watched him standing in the moonlight, naked, aroused, his skin gleaming darkly. He lay down with her, saying nothing, taking off her kimono and kissing her body all over with fiery kisses. There was a raw urgency in his touch, and a tide of mindless longing swept over her. She put her arms around him, pressing herself against him, wanting him, needing him. If only he would speak—say something, anything. She needed to hear his voice, hear words of love and desire. But he was nothing but a silent shape, a demon in the dark night, playing with her body, driving her mind blank of all thought. There was no past, no future, only a wild elemental force driving her onward into a storm of fire.

Sand and sky and sea and wind, all blended in a whirlwind of sensation, earthy and eternal like the forces within them. Eve felt his hand search her body, warm and urgent. She felt the wind cool her heated skin. Beyond his dark, shadowed face, she saw the brightness of the stars. She heard his ragged breathing, and in the background the gentle lapping of the waves.

A blazing fire, more pain than comfort, raged between them. She was lost in a sea of nameless emotions, her senses reeling with the sudden onslaught. A frantic passion consumed them, a primitive play of hands and mouths and heated bodies that went on and on in savage silence until the frenzy shattered and stilled the storm of fire.

She lay motionless in the sand, her breathing ragged, her heart pounding. Parker rolled away from her, not speaking, not touching. He flung his arm over his eyes, as if he did not want to see her, wanted to block out what had just happened. She looked at him, her throat clogged with tears. Sand stuck to his damp body, glistening in the silver light.

Eve glanced up at the stars, shivering, her throat aching. There'd been fire, but no warmth. Passion, but no love. But how could she expect love from Parker?

An eternity later, she sat up. She wasn't sure if she had slept or not. She looked up at the Plantation great house with its magnificent backdrop of deep green jungle-covered mountains, seeing behind them the rising sun coloring the sky in crystal-pure pastels.

I don't hate you, he'd said. Then what did he feel for her? She shivered suddenly, thinking of the way they had made love. Never before had it been like this, and she wasn't sure if she ever wanted it like this again. She looked down at him. He'd rolled away from her, the upper part of him lying on her kimono, the lower in the sand. His face was turned away from her.

Her heart contracted in pain. There was nothing left of the magic they had once shared. There was not even a sense of intimacy, of connection. Parker lay two feet away from her—not a big distance, but it might as well have been the Grand Canyon.

She felt a surge of despair. Why had she let this happen? Why had she let sentimentality and physical need take over? The dream was lost and she would never recapture it, no matter how hard she tried.

She got up, picked up his T-shirt and pulled it on over her head. It had the clean, familiar scent of his body, and tears welled up in her eyes. She left him to lie on the kimono and slowly made her way back to the cottage. He didn't follow her. Maybe he was sleeping. Maybe he really didn't know she was leaving.

She lay down on her bed, not bothering to shower or brush off the sand, watching the sky grow lighter, hearing the birds greet the morning.

Finally she got up, had a shower and had the kitchen send some breakfast. She forced down some slices of mango and papaya and had a cup of *café au lait*.

The phone rang. It was her father calling, saying he was back from London where he'd been for the past week.

He wanted to know how she was. She sounded tired, he said. Was she getting enough sleep? Was she sick? Was everything all right?

"Of course everything's all right," she lied. "What's the matter with you, Dad?" He seemed overly concerned, and it baffled her.

"I hear Parker Adams is staying at the Plantation," he said.

Eve was baffled no more. "That's right, Dad." She wasn't surprised he knew. One way or another, he always found out everything. She only hoped he didn't know about the scene on the beach last night.

"Why didn't you let me know?" he demanded. "I'll have him off the island tomorrow if you want."

"Dad! I can take care of myself. Please don't intervene! I'm not a girl any more!"

He sighed. "I know, Princess."

"Just leave him be. I'm fine." The lie of the century, but she was going to handle this herself. She didn't need a Big Daddy to bail her out every time she had a problem.

"Okay, okay. It was just a question."

"How was your trip?" she asked, changing the subject. They talked for a while.

"When are you coming back home?" he asked at last. "Or are you planning to stay there for the rest of your life? You've got to make some plans one of these days, Eve."

"I have a plan." It had been germinating in her head for a while. Maybe this was the time to test the waters and get her father's reaction.

"And what's that, may I ask?"

She laughed. "I want you to help me. I want you to find me a house in Philadelphia—a big house." She began to tell him of her plan.

He was not enthusiastic, she could tell, but that was no surprise. "Princess, you're off your rocker," he said succinctly. "You have no idea what you're getting yourself into."

"I know exactly what I'm getting myself into. I also know I'll need your help."

He sighed heavily. "I'm not going to talk you out of this, am I?"

"No, Dad, you're not."

He sighed again. "Okay, okay, I'll find you a house."

Eve smiled into the phone. "And will you help me with the rest?"

"When did I ever say no to you?" The wistful tone to his voice surprised her.

When she replaced the receiver, her eye caught Parker's T-shirt. Maybe she should bring it back. Quickly she picked it up, folded it and made her way to his cottage.

He was sitting at his desk, working on the computer, his back turned to her. She listened for a moment to the fast, dull tic-tac of the keys, gathering strength. She wished her heart would calm down.

"Good morning," she said.

Parker turned in his chair. "Good morning." His face was inscrutable, his voice expressionless.

"I brought you back your T-shirt." She put it on a chair. "Do you have my kimono?"

"It's over there." He waved at a pile of cushions in the corner.

She wasn't sure what she had hoped for. Some warmth, something to indicate that their lovemaking had had some meaning. Something, anything to take away the empty feel of desolation inside her.

He might still want her physically, but in the light of day all he could think of was what she had done to him five years ago.

She couldn't even blame him. He was not a man to forget easily. But for a moment he had forgotten, overwhelmed by memories and need. Once, a long time ago, he had loved her, although now it was difficult to understand.

"Parker?"

He didn't look up.

"I'm talking to you! Will you please look at me?"

He sighed impatiently and looked at her, eyes without expression. "What do you want?"

"Last night you told me you didn't hate me." Her voice shook. "What exactly does that mean?"

"Oh, for God's sake!" he burst out. "Forget about last night. It was a mistake."

Eve's heart sank. "Thanks very much," she said bitterly. "And if I'm pregnant, I'll write it off as a mistake too, right?"

His body grew rigid, then he scraped back his chair and got up. "Get out of here," he said viciously. "Just get the hell out of here!"

She turned blindly, clutching the kimono to her chest.

How she made it back to her cottage without falling was a miracle.

In the bedroom she took out a small case and threw in some clothes. She had to get away from the Plantation, away from Parker. She could not tolerate seeing him, not even from a distance. She called Daniella, who said of course she could come and stay, as long as she wanted. She'd love the company and there was plenty of room.

Eve drove over immediately, finding Daniella waiting for her with a pot of coffee.

Eve sat down on the couch and covered her face with her hands. "Oh, God," she moaned, "I don't know what to do!"

"It's this Parker Adams, isn't it?" Daniella poured them each a cup of coffee.

"Yes." Eve lowered her hands and took a deep breath. "He's not married. That woman who was with him isn't his wife."

"Oh? You could have fooled me," Daniella said dryly. "They sure seemed to know each other well."

"They do." Eve picked up the cup and took a sip of the coffee. It was very hot and very strong. "She's his son's mother's sister. His sister-in-law, if he'd been married to his son's mother, which he wasn't."

Daniella raised her eyebrows. "How complicated is this story?"

In spite of herself, Eve managed a wan smile. "Actually it's extremely simple." She swallowed some more coffee, hoping it would give her strength. Then she began to recount the story from the beginning, her voice toneless. It was easier the second time, and she was grateful Daniella didn't interrupt her.

"I thought I'd learned to live with it and put it all behind me, but then, when he came here..." Eve closed her eyes. "It wasn't true. I'd only buried it." She looked into her cup. "I still feel this terrible guilt. I have so many regrets." She swallowed hard, blinking at her tears.

"When did you find out he wasn't married?" asked Daniella.

"Last night." She bit her lower lip. "Yesterday was the seventeenth, our wedding day five years ago. He came to my cottage at night." The coffee cup trembled in her hand. "We made love." She closed her eyes. "It was... awful."

Daniella's eyes widened. "Awful? What do you mean? Did he hurt you?"

Eve shook her head. "No, no. It was just... bad. It was a terrible mistake. He hates me." She put the cup on the table and covered her face with her hands. Her voice choking, she told Daniella what had happened that morning, about Parker's rage.

"I suppose," Daniella said quietly, "he's having trouble with his own emotions. Anger isn't always what it seems, you know."

Eve picked up her cup and took a drink of coffee. "I've never seen him so angry. He...he doesn't lose control."

"But he did this morning. That must mean something."

"Yes," Eve said bitterly. "He hates me."

Eve moved through the day on automatic pilot. It was Saturday, and she ran some errands and spent a couple of hours with Fiona going over the adoption paperwork and reading family studies that had been sent to them from Canada. She was back at the Penbrooke villa in the early afternoon and she spent another hour emptying her soul to Daniella. Now that she'd started telling all, there seemed to be no end to it. Daniella listened patiently, sipping a glass of soursop juice, making a comment now and then.

Finally, with a big sigh, Eve stopped talking. "God, I must be a bore! Where's Marc?"

"He went scuba diving with friends." Daniella looked at her watch. "He should be back any minute."

A couple of hours later Fish flew the three of them to Trinidad for the weekend. There was a party to celebrate the opening of a painting exhibition of one of Daniella's friends and Daniella had persuaded Eve to come with them. Eve always enjoyed Trinidad's dynamic, cosmopolitan atmosphere, and the party was alive and festive. Talking and laughing, she felt herself begin to come back to life. It was good to laugh, it was good to feel lighthearted, if only for a short while.

Fish flew them back on Sunday afternoon and on Monday morning Eve went back to St. Mary's. After the weekend the children were happy to see her. There was an atmosphere of excitement about the place, because today there would be a party for Rosie. Today Rosie was leaving.

At eleven the adoptive parents arrived, nervous and excited. The mother took Rosie in her arms and the baby smiled at her delightedly. She was oblivious to the importance of the day, or the importance of the two people eagerly watching her.

Dr. Kimmel and Father Matthias arrived at the same time to take part in the festivities. It was a wonderful party, with cake and laughter and lots of tears. The nuns were crying, Eve was crying, the new mother was crying. The new father smiled bravely, swallowing a lot.

When they were ready to leave, Eve hugged Rosie, holding her soft, warm baby body against her for a moment. "Goodbye, sweetheart," she whispered in her ear. "Have a happy life."

It took a while to get the children under control after that, but once the little ones had been put to bed for a nap, some semblance of order was restored.

Eve left shortly before four, and as she stepped out of the building she noticed another Mini-Moke parked next to hers.

Sitting in the driver's seat was Parker.

CHAPTER SEVEN

EVE felt her heart turn over, and stopped, her feet rooted to the ground. Her first impulse was to turn around and go back inside, but on second thoughts she stayed where she was. It wouldn't help to go inside. If Parker wanted to see her, he would see her. He'd simply follow her in, and she had no desire to have the children and the nuns be witness to whatever might occur.

She took a deep breath and, steeling herself, walked up to the car, aware of him watching her limp along.

He leaped lithely out of his Moke and leaned casually against it. "Eve? Can we talk?"

The keys dug into her palm. "I've nothing to say to you."

"I have something to say to you."

She looked at him coldly. "You've said it all. You told me to get the hell away from you, and I did. Now return the favor and stay the hell away from me!"

She heard her voice tremble with anger. She had wanted to be cool and in control. She didn't want to let him see how much his rage had shaken her.

His face was pale. "I wasn't myself. I want you to know how sorry I am for what happened and for what I said to you. It was unforgivable."

She gave him a stony stare, saying nothing.

Parker closed his eyes briefly. "I don't know what happened to me. I was possessed." He raked his hands through his hair, dark eyes meeting hers. "I apologize, Eve."

113

Still she said nothing. She saw the tension in the hard lines of his body, the tightening of his jaw.

He jammed his hands in his shorts' pockets. "I'm trying to apologize, Eve! The least you can do is acknowledge it in some way!"

"All right." She looked at him coolly. "Apology accepted."

He rubbed his forehead. "Eve..."

"What do you want from me?" she asked with angry impatience. "We made a mistake—fine. You got mad—okay. You apologized and I accepted. Case closed." She opened the car door, sat down in the driver's seat and slammed the windowless door with finality.

Parker moved closer, hands grasping the top rail. His dark eyes bored into hers. "If you're pregnant, the case is not closed."

Eve's heart lurched at the words. She fought to keep her voice steady. "I'm a big girl, I'll handle it." She didn't even want to think about it, much less talk about it.

"We're both responsible, damn it!"

"Thank you," she said coldly, "for your emancipated views. I'll keep you posted." She was too angry to be reasonable. She took her key, attempting to put it in the ignition, but her hand was shaking so much, she missed. He grabbed the keys from her fingers.

"You damn well will! Don't for a minute think I'll let this slide by!"

"Of course not," she said caustically.

Anger stiffened his jaw. "When will you know?"

She shrugged. "In four or five days." At least she wouldn't have the uncertainty hanging over her head for weeks.

Parker closed his eyes and sighed. "Let me know, please."

Eve felt suddenly drained of all emotion. "I will." She held out her hand. "May I have my keys back?"

He handed them to her and she took them without their fingers touching.

She drove back to the Penbrooke villa, trying not to feel, not to think.

Yet when she and Daniella sat on the veranda with tea and coconut cake, she felt the irrepressible need to talk, to let it all out, to somehow exorcise the pain with words.

"You know, Eve," Daniella said carefully, "I'm getting tired of hearing you beat yourself up. All you keep saying is that you were such a horrible selfish witch."

"Well, I was. I did a terrible thing."

"Eve," Daniella said patiently, "there comes a time when you have to accept the past for what it is and forgive yourself."

Eve gave a bitter little laugh. "Forgive myself?"

"Yes! What matters is not what and who you *were*, but what and who you *are now*. It happened five years ago, when you were young and immature and too indulged. We all have to start young and learn to grow up. Not everybody gets lessons the way you did."

"You were never young and immature."

Daniella shrugged. "In my own way, I had to grow up too."

Daniella's lessons had been of a different nature, but she had passed them with flying colors as far as Eve could tell. Daniella had never been young. Growing up poor sometimes did that for you. Having a sick mother, no father and a drunk grandfather who beat you up taught you how to grow up fast.

"You have to forgive yourself." The words kept coming back to her during the next few days. She struggled with them, knowing the truth of them. She knew she was no longer the girl she had once been. She was a new person with new insights and better priorities. She thought of Daniella, who was her friend; of Nick. Neither one had judged her. She thought of Fiona who still didn't know. Maybe Fiona would not judge her either. She thought of the children who loved her. And as the days passed she felt a measure of her self-confidence return. She was a worthy person. A person who deserved love, not contempt.

She struggled through long, sleepless nights. It was not easy to come to terms with the person she had once been. It was not easy to forgive that selfish little rich girl who had thought the world owed her everything.

She stayed with Daniella and Marc for the rest of the week, then spent the weekend with Fiona and David and their three children. Joshua was a guest at the estate as well, and he greeted her with a wide grin, asking where she'd been, saying he'd missed her at the beach.

"I was visiting friends," Eve answered, touched by his interest.

"It's Kevin's birthday on Monday," he told her, "and they're having a party and I can stay till Tuesday!"

"You're lucky." She smiled at his eager face. She felt an urge to hug him, but didn't. At St. Mary's she was always hugging the children. They needed so much to be held and loved. But Joshua had a father and an aunt and loving grandparents. Joshua didn't need her hugs.

One reason she'd come to the estate was to tell Fiona about Parker and what had happened five years ago. Fiona was her friend too, and it seemed important to come clean, not to have any more secrets.

"I think Daniella is right," Fiona said after she had silently listened to the story. "You have to let the past be the past and go on with your life. You're a terrific person, Eve, and what happened in the past isn't going to change my opinion of you.''

Eve was glad she had told Fiona. It felt good to have the support of her friends.

She left on Sunday evening. It was time to go back to the Plantation and face Parker again.

''Hello, Parker.''

He put his coffee cup down and for a moment he looked at her silently. ''You're back,'' he stated evenly.

''I needed some time to get things into perspective.'' She felt calm now, calmer than she had felt in weeks, as if some heavy weight had been lifted from her.

It was a glorious morning, as were so many on the island. The sun had just come up and the world was cool and green and fragrant. She had returned from the Penbrooke villa the night before and she had awakened early. She had gone in search of Parker, finding him at the lower terrace of the great house where breakfast was served. Crisp pink and white tablecloths covered the small tables. Birds chirped in the rich green foliage surrounding the terrace. A blue butterfly fluttered above the violet bougainvillaea blossoms.

Parker pointed at a chair. ''Sit down. Have some breakfast.''

''Thank you.'' Eve sat down and poured a cup of coffee. Mercifully, her hand was steady. She looked up, seeing his face, the tired lines etched beside his mouth. ''I came to tell you that I'm not pregnant,'' she said.

Relief flared in his eyes. ''Thank you for telling me.'' He put his fork down. ''It was stupid and irresponsible to take such a risk,'' he said quietly. ''I'd lost my mind— I don't know how else to explain it. I'm sorry.''

"It's over now." She took a sip from the coffee. "I was at the Keatings' estate for the weekend. Joshua's having a great time." Shifting the conversation to less dangerous ground seemed a good idea.

Parker's mouth quirked. "He and Kevin are big buddies."

"I'm glad he found someone to play with." She put her cup down. "We're taking the kids to Pirate Beach the day after tomorrow. It's a public beach, and there are fishermen there and boats and an old pirates' fort. I thought Joshua might like to see it."

"Don't you have enough on your hands with the others?"

She shrugged. "Joshua's no trouble."

He held her gaze. "I'm sure he'd be delighted. He'll be back here tomorrow."

Eve glanced at her watch. "I think I'd better go." She came to her feet. "Thanks."

As she walked to the parking lot behind the great house building, she wondered what she'd been thanking him for. Not for the coffee, surely. Maybe because he'd offered it to her. A small peace offering, perhaps?

The wind was cool on her face as she drove to the orphanage. She passed a farmer on a donkey and a woman carrying a basket of pineapples on her head. She drove slowly, passing them carefully, still thinking about Parker, wondering what he was thinking about her.

His anger had cooled. He'd been more himself—calm and under control, the man she recognized. Eve thought of the fury she'd seen in him and shivered. That night on the beach—what ghosts had they been laying to rest? Or had it been more than that?

Her father called again on Tuesday night. "Eve? Is that you?"

"Yes, it is. How are you, Dad?"

"What's the matter? You sound funny."

"It's just the line, Dad. I'm fine."

"What's going on?" His voice was insistent. "Is it Parker? Is he still there?"

"You *know* he's still here." He would have made it his business to know, she was certain. No doubt the manager was under orders to call the moment Parker left. Her father would know in Philadelphia before she did.

"How is it between you two?" he wanted to know.

"How's *what* between us, Dad? He's working. He's busy. I haven't seen him for two days."

"I wasn't asking if he was busy. I was asking how it was between you two. If there's any problem, I'll have him kicked off the island."

"Dad!" Eve gave an exasperated sigh. "Will you stop this? I hardly see him. I'm at St. Mary's all day. I'm busy."

"You're avoiding the issue, Princess."

She closed her eyes and bit her tongue, hard. She expelled her breath slowly. "What is it you want to hear? That Parker and I are killing each other off or that we've fallen madly in love again?"

"Have you?"

She slipped along the wall and sat down on the cold tile floor. "He did that once, Dad. He's not going to make the same mistake twice. You know Parker as well as I do. I'm not a good risk proposition, and you don't invest in something that's not a good risk." Putting it in financial terms made it easier to say, less personal somehow.

He gave a muffled curse. "Who says you're not a good risk?"

"Oh, come on, Dad, let's not start this! Tell me about you."

"I've been thinking I'd come over for a couple of days. I'll be in Sydney for ten days, and after that I have to go to Rio. I thought I'd stop by for a few days on the way over."

"That would be great, Dad. Haven't seen you for ages, it seems."

"Have you got someone to take your place yet?"

She laughed. "Oh, Dad! The Government needs to make a formal request for a volunteer. I've been after Robertson for months now, trying to make him see the need. He figures as long as no one's there, I'll stay anyway, so he's in no hurry."

"And how right he is!" There was humor in his voice.

"Well, I'm not leaving here until I'm satisfied there's someone to take over. These kids need all the help they can get, and I refuse to use them as pawns in some stupid game of politics!"

He laughed. "Don't get mad at me—I'm doing my part. I've been looking for a house. Something may come up pretty soon. It's a building that's used as office space now, but it used to be a family house. It'll need renovation, but so will any of them. If that one doesn't work, we'll find another."

Eve smiled. She could never stay angry with her father for long. "What would I do without you, Dad?"

"I wonder," he said dryly. "What I'm asking myself is how I always let myself get dragged into your little schemes."

She laughed. "It's simple, Dad. I'm irresistible."

"It'd be good if Parker thought that too."

She let out a long, suffering sigh. "Dad! Don't start now!"

It wasn't until later that his remark finally sank in and a sudden suspicion began to lurk around in her thoughts.

It'd be good if Parker thought that too.

Did her father want her to get back with Parker? And the next question: did her father have anything to do with Parker's being here on the island? She shrugged the thought away. She couldn't iamgine how he could.

Eve watched the fishermen mend their nets, heard the children's laughter. Several brightly painted fishing boats were pulled up on the beach, the orange, blue, turquoise and yellow making a cheerful picture against the backdrop of deep blue sky.

Now and then, when it could be arranged, the children at the orphanage spent a few hours at Pirate Beach where they swam, played in the sand and watched the fishermen work on their boats and nets. The Plantation donated picnic lunches and vans to drive the children to and from the beach. It was not an easy excursion, with several of the children unable to move by themselves, but the joy they found in the trip was worth any effort. Joshua proved to be invaluable help.

Eve sat in the sand in the shade of a casuarina with one of the babies in her lap, watching Joshua play at the water's edge with Timothy and Winston. He was so good with the kids, it amazed her. Lunch was over, and he'd helped, unasked, making sure everyone had what he or she needed.

As they were about to pack up, Parker appeared at the beach, wearing white shorts and a blue sports shirt.

"Joshua was so excited about this fort, I thought I'd come and have a look," he said as he reached the place where she was sitting.

Her heart beat uneasily at the sight of him. "It's just a ruin, but it's kind of spooky inside," she said.

He sat down next to her, looking at the baby in her lap, who stared at him with big brown eyes. Tobias was a beautiful little baby with two club feet. He'd been at the orphanage for four months now, abandoned as a newborn baby at the steps of the Ark of Love Catholic Church.

Parker stroked the chubby little leg. "He won't be able to walk," he said.

"Not like this, no."

"What's going to happen to him?"

"We've found an adoptive family for him in Toronto. We've been able to speed everything up because of the medical problems. They're coming next week to pick him up." She hugged him to her. "He'll have to have several operations and braces and special shoes, but it can be fixed."

Tobias gave her a wide smile, as if he understood what she had just said. She smiled back at him, nuzzling his neck. "You're going to have so much fun with your new brother and sister, aren't you? They'll help you practice walking and teach you how to ride a bike and tell you how to get into trouble." She tickled his ribs. "You probably won't need any help getting into trouble. You'll know how to do that all by yourself."

He gave a delighted little baby laugh, then promptly got the hiccups.

Parker watched him with a smile. "Cheerful, isn't he?"

Eve nodded. "And tough, I bet. He'll be playing soccer by the time he's three." She shaded her eyes and scanned the water's edge. The children were behaving. The nuns were paddling in the water, having as much fun as the children. The news that it was time to leave would not be greeted with much enthusiasm.

"How's Joshua been?" asked Parker.

She looked back at him and smiled. "He's been great with the kids. He doesn't seem to feel awkward at all with them. He's a super boy, Parker. You should be proud of him." She looked away, suddenly embarrassed.

"I am," he said quietly.

Eve bit her lip, feeling awkward. Five years ago she could not have envisaged that she'd have this discussion with Parker, telling him he should be proud of his son. She pushed the memories back, searching desperately for another topic.

Joshua came running toward them. "Hey, Dad! Did you see the fort? It's awesome! You wanna come and see it inside?"

Eve watched as the two plodded through the sand to the rocky steps leading up to the fort. Father and son. She felt a lump in her throat. They would have been hers if... Oh, stop it! Stop it! she told herself fiercely.

Five years. Wasted. Lost forever. She could have been Joshua's mother. She could have been Parker's wife. Such pain, such regret.

No. She would have been no good as a mother, or a wife, then. She'd been far too selfish to face up to those responsibilities and demands. She'd been far too involved with her own desires and needs—the things she wanted to do, the things she wanted to have. She didn't want to listen to childish chatter and read fairy tales. It all spelled boring with a capital "B."

But there was another reason she'd not been able to deal with the existence of Parker's son. The reality of a son meant the reality of another woman in his life. She had known, of course, that there had been other women, but he never talked about them, at least not much, and she'd never thought about them. To her they were not real. Now, with Joshua, it was different. Every time she looked at the boy, she would be faced with the mother.

A woman Parker had loved, a woman with whom he'd shared a bed, with whom he'd made love...

She hadn't wanted to think about that. Parker was hers, hers alone, or so she'd wanted it to be. She hadn't wanted to be reminded day after day that there'd once been another woman. Even if that woman had never been his wife. Even if that woman was now dead.

Despite all the terrible strain, she had sensed in Parker a certain delight at the knowledge that he had a son. A son who was not her own, not their son, but someone else's. It was as if someone else had stolen her dreams, and her life lay shattered at her feet.

It had taken a tragedy to make her grow up.

The baby squirmed in her arms and grabbed for her nose.

"I hope you'll have more sense than I do when you grow up," she said, hugging him. "When you find love, don't give it up for anything. Okay?"

A hiccup cut short his smile.

For the next few days, everything seemed calm and quiet. Sometimes they talked, but nothing very significant was said. Joshua had made another friend at the Plantation, Erasmus's son Nelson. He'd been hanging around at the kitchen, waiting for his father to get off work, when Joshua, on one of his explorations, had discovered him. Parker had acquired a guest pass for the child so the two boys could play together, which would work as long as they behaved themselves and did not bother the other guests.

On Saturday morning Eve went to the pool for a swim. The Italian *contessa* was doing laps. An Arab sheikh, dressed in wide flowered swimming shorts with his big belly bulging over the waistband, was eating a solitary breakfast at one of the tables. Without his headdress and flowing robes he looked like a friendly neighborhood plumber. He'd come to the Plantation with an entourage of several very flashy people, all of whom presumably were still in bed.

At the deep end Parker was giving Joshua diving lessons. Joshua waved Eve over enthusiastically, and she dived into the water and swam up to them.

She returned their good morning and watched while Joshua showed off his diving skill. "Hey, you're doing great!" she smiled, and he glowed with pride.

She went off to swim a few laps. Swimming was good exercise for her leg and she could still do it with relative ease, if not with the same streamlined movements of before. Later, as she sat on a lounger drying off in the sun, Parker came over and joined her.

He rubbed his left shoulder, wincing as if it hurt him, then glanced at her leg. "You really don't care about people seeing your leg, do you?"

She raised her brows. "Should I?"

He waved his hand impatiently. "Of course you *shouldn't*."

"But you're wondering why I don't?"

"Yes."

"Well, I did, in the beginning. I didn't want anybody to see me like this. I wasn't used to people looking at me with that *look* in their eyes, you know, as if it embarrassed them, or as if they felt sorry for me. I hated that." People had never looked at her like that. They'd looked at her with envy or desire or admiration, never with pity. "Then I got mad at myself. If I had to worry what people thought of me, I was just going to make myself miserable. It was too hard. So I decided just to pretend there wasn't anything wrong with me, and if people had a problem with the way I looked, then that was their problem, not mine."

Parker studied her for a moment, brown eyes pensive. "I bet it wasn't as easy as all that."

She gave a half smile. "Well, maybe not." She'd cried a few tears of frustration.

He held her eyes. "I admire your courage," he said.

Eve inclined her head in mock graciousness. "Thank you, sir. Now why don't you get us a cup of coffee?"

Every morning a table was set up near the pool with coffee, juice, fruit and sweet rolls so guests could help themselves. If a more elaborate breakfast was required it would gladly be delivered.

Parker got up and brought back coffee and almond croissants and placed them on a small table between the two loungers. Handing her a cup, he caught her eyes. "How about dinner tonight?"

The question caught her by surprise and she didn't answer immediately.

He gave her a questioning look. "Is that a strange request?"

"No, no. I just wasn't expecting it, I suppose."

His mouth quirked. "Will you have dinner with me tonight, please?"

Eve nodded, smiling. "I'd like that." She felt a small thrill of anticipation. How many times in the past had they had dinner together? Many, many times. But this was different, very different.

"I'd like to try a place other than the Plantation," said Parker. "Any suggestions?"

"There's nothing around with *haute cuisine*," she said. "If you're up to plain island food, we can go to the Sugar Bay Hotel in town." She bit her lip and looked down at her plate with the untouched croissant. "The place where the cocktail party was."

"Would you like that, or would you rather stay here?"

"No, I like island food. They have a big dinner buffet on Saturdays, and a steel band and dancing afterward. I can't dance, but I can watch. There's a nice atmosphere with a lot of local color, and it's fun."

He nodded. "Sounds good. I'm ready for a change of scene. Let's go for it."

She looked out over the pool, seeing Joshua's head bob up and down in the water. "What about Joshua? One of the room girls can baby-sit—they do sometimes. They like the extra money."

He nodded. "I know. Carlotta watches him in the daytime when I have to go into Port Royal for meetings, but he won't be here tonight." He grinned. "He's going home to the village with Nelson and Erasmus this afternoon. He'll be staying the night and the kids are going to sleep on the back veranda in hammocks. Imagine the adventure!"

Eve laughed. "Boy, wait till he can tell his friends in Philadelphia!"

Joshua might be bored on the Plantation, but he didn't miss a chance for entertainment when it presented itself. She wondered what he would think of the small village house where Erasmus and his family lived, and of the food they'd eat. Children were not known for their culinary adventurousness, and goat stew or curried conch, nutritious food though it might be, might be hard to get down for an eight-year-old from Philadelphia.

Eve finished her coffee and croissant. "I'd better go now—duty calls."

He frowned. "You work on Saturdays?"

"Not at St. Mary's. I go to the Keatings' to do adoption paperwork with Fiona and plan strategies to deal with our friend Darnell Robertson." She came to her feet and wrapped her towel around her waist. "I'll see you tonight."

"Seven-thirty all right?"

She nodded. Parker's eyes held hers and she felt herself grow oddly light. She dropped her gaze and moved away, making her way back to her cottage along the winding path.

He had asked her out to dinner. He was going to spend the evening with her voluntarily. They were going to eat together and talk like two people who wanted to be in each other's company.

She couldn't believe this was happening. Not after that night on the beach and the emotions and memories they had stirred up in each other. Yet she had sensed a change in him in the last few days. She felt a tiny flicker of hope.

She couldn't wait till tonight.

CHAPTER EIGHT

Eve dressed with excessive care. She even had her nails and hair done at the Plantation beauty salon. It really was necessary anyway, she rationalized. She hadn't been paying much attention to her nails lately and her hair needed a trim. While she was at it, she decided to have a facial as well. It was nice to be pampered, to just lie back and have someone massage your face and smother it in creams and lotions.

She picked out a white floral print dress that looked deceptively simple and could go many places. She could wear it and not feel overdressed for the Sugar Bay Hotel. The colorful fabric and playful lines of the dress made it fit perfectly with the island style. She let her hair hang loose in a casual, curly style, tucked back on one side with a large comb.

She was ready when Parker arrived at seven-thirty sharp. He was always on time. He was casually dressed in a pair of light tailored trousers and a striped, open-necked shirt with short sleeves. Making distinctive fashion statements was not in his conservative character, but he always looked comfortably secure with himself no matter what he wore. It was this understated self-confidence, the cool composure, that gave him such a strong male appeal. Here was a man who knew himself and had no need to show off or impress anyone. His bearing, the athletic grace of his tall body, and his dark, aloof expression were enough to make people look twice.

"I'm ready," she said, picking up her clutch bag from the table.

His gaze lingered on her for a moment. "You look beautiful, Eve."

She smiled. "Thank you." She would have liked to be able to sweep elegantly out onto the terrace, as she would have done in the past, but sweeping elegantly was something that was no longer possible, so she hobbled out with her chin in the air and her shoulders straight.

He adjusted his long-legged stride to an easy stroll so she wouldn't have trouble keeping up with him. It was dark, with small lights discreetly hidden in the foliage lighting the path.

They drove his Mini-Moke into Port Royal, which wasn't a long drive, and they talked casually, almost like friendly strangers.

Maybe that's what we are now, Eve thought. How well do we really know each other after five years? Yet he hadn't changed much, not in anything that she had noticed. It was she who had changed. She wondered if Parker was aware of it, if this dinner was an attempt to get to know her better. Was he willing to forget the past and start over?

It was a thought that made her shiver with fearful hope.

They arrived at the Sugar Bay Hotel, hearing the music spilling into the street. The place was alive with people, mostly islanders with the odd foreigner taking in the local color.

"Fiona and David are here," Parker told her as they entered the main room. Tables had been set up on one side, the other cleared to make a place for dancing.

She looked around in surprise. "Really? I didn't know they were planning to come. Fiona didn't mention it this morning."

David had spotted them too, and the two came over, Fiona looking apologetic. "I hope you don't mind our

being here, but after you mentioned that you were going
I thought it was such a good idea. I haven't been off the
island now for six months and I was going stir crazy,"
she complained. "I wanted to dance. So I made him
take me here."

David rolled his eyes. "What I don't do to keep my
spouse happy!"

"Don't you like to dance?" asked Eve.

"I'm on my feet all day. I want to put them up at
night."

"He's feeling his age," Fiona said sweetly.

They moved through the buffet line together. The
spread was quite different from the gourmet fare of the
Plantation, but looked nonetheless very appetizing. Eve
scanned the dishes—deep-fried flying fish, turtle stew,
bluggo in coconut sauce, fried plantain, pickled breadfruit, tania fritters, cornmeal-coconut bread and a variety
of salads and other dishes. She took a little bit of each,
ending up with a plate with much too much food.

At David's suggestion, they all shared a table. Eve
didn't mind; it made it easier to talk. She felt oddly insecure about being alone with Parker for any length of
time. The conversation flowed smoothly enough—David,
with his quirky sense of humor, made it easy.

After a dessert of nutmeg ice cream, Fiona pulled
David out of his chair. "Come on, old man, let's dance
it all off!"

He obeyed with a groan. Eve watched the dancers,
recognizing among them Darnell Robertson, the Minister
of Social Services, Child Welfare, Cultural Affairs and
Sports. He was a good dancer, as was his pretty young
wife, who had done her hair up in masses of tiny beaded
braids in some African or black American imitation.
Mostly the islanders had no-nonsense short-cropped

hairdos. Mrs. Robertson had been abroad, as was opulently obvious.

A waiter poured them another cup of strong island coffee.

"Tell me about your project," she said to Parker. "I've been wondering how it would work. There aren't that many people here who know how to work on a computer." It was a safe subject, and she needed some safe conversation.

"People will be trained on the job, at least initially. It's very routine work and it shouldn't be difficult." He went on talking about meetings he'd had with the Government people and local businessmen, about the company lawyer who was arriving on the island the next morning to handle the legal parts of the business plan.

Eve listened, savoring the rich sound of his voice, watching the familiar features of his face, feeling the stirring of a restless longing. She watched his strong brown hands playing absently with a spoon. He had good hands, with long, lean fingers and neat square nails. She wished he'd reach out and take her hand. She wished she had the courage to touch him. How odd to think she was afraid to touch him, this man who had almost been her husband.

The music came to a stop and the leader of the band announced a short break. The dancers moved back to their seats, and David sagged down in his chair, panting like a dog in a desert. "Drink, drink," he whispered hoarsely.

"Can I get you a glass of water?" Parker asked solicitously, winking at Fiona.

David looked pained and Parker laughed. "How about a rum punch, double strength? Maybe that will make a dancer out of you." He beckoned a waiter, and soon they all had a drink in front of them.

"Why don't you dance with Fiona?" Eve said to Parker when the band started up again. "Give the poor weary farmer a rest."

He gave her a searching look. "You don't mind?"

"Why would I mind? You like dancing. I have absolutely no martyrdom tendencies, so go ahead. If Fiona will have you, of course." She gave Fiona a questioning look.

"Please!" Fiona begged. "Dance with me!"

The two of them went to the crowded dance floor, and Eve watched them for a moment. She wasn't a martyr, but she couldn't help feeling a sense of loss. She had liked dancing herself. She wouldn't have minded at all now dancing with Parker, to have his arms around her, to move with him to the music. She took a drink and swallowed away the feeling.

David gave her a grateful smile. "Thank you! You saved me. That woman has too much energy for her own good."

"Go ahead, blame it all on her," Eve said without sympathy. "You're a terrible spoilsport, David Keating."

He grinned his boyish grin. "I like giving her a hard time." His blue eyes gleamed devilishly. "Later, when we get home, she'll make me beg for forgiveness."

Eve laughed, shaking her head. "The games people play!"

It was a fun evening. Several people came up to their table to say hello. Darnell Robertson and his fashionable wife joined them for a drink and he too was roped into dancing with Fiona. Before they took off for the dance floor, Eve winked at Fiona. "We need that Government request for a volunteer," she said in a loud stage whisper. "Work on him, okay?"

Darnell Robertson gave Eve a look of dignified reproach. "I didn't hear that."

Eve smiled sweetly. "You didn't hear what?"

After the Robertsons had left their table and David was struggling himself through one more dance with Fiona, Eve found herself alone with Parker again.

"You know a lot of people here," he stated.

"I suppose I do. It's a miracle Darnell still speaks to me. Every time he sees me coming, I fully expect him to jump out of the nearest window, screaming."

Parker laughed. "You're very persistent, but I already knew that."

She shrugged. "I've got to be." Nobody else would be. Not the nuns, who were sweet and caring, but who had no idea how to go about getting help from the Government.

"Have you settled on the island permanently?" he asked, toying with his glass.

She laughed. "Can you picture me here for the rest of my life? Think of it—me at sixty-five, gray and wrinkled and still working at St. Mary's and doing battle with Darnell Robertson."

"They'll write articles about you in the church magazines."

Eve groaned. "Oh, please!" She could imagine the headings: "Crippled Spinster Dedicates Life to Island Orphans."

Parker gave a crooked smile. "All right, so that's not what you had in mind. What are your plans, then?"

"I'm trying to get Robertson to put in a formal request for a Peace Corps volunteer, or one from the Canadian or British volunteer services. When we have someone to take over for me, I can think of leaving, but not before that."

"What are you going to do then?" he asked.

She smiled. "I'm going to buy myself a big house in Philadelphia."

His face was carefully blank. "I see."

She doubted that he did.

He eyed her curiously. "Are you going to work?"

"Yes. I'm going to start my own non-profit-making organization, bringing children from St. Mary's over for medical treatment they can't get here. When they're better they'll go back to St. Mary's, or on to adoptive homes. Maybe we can take care of other children as well, through the mission hospital, or from the other small islands. We'll see."

"That's quite an ambitious project," he said carefully. "I can see all kinds of bureaucratic problems and pitfalls."

"Oh, yes, I know, but I'm going to make it work. I've got my own money to start with and I've got my father roped in, and we'll find other sources. He's got lots of connections."

"What does he think of this?"

She laughed, tucking a loose curl behind her ear. "What do you think he thinks? He thinks I'm nuts."

"But you're his princess and you get whatever you want." It was a statement, not a question.

She didn't look at him. "Right."

"Does he still call you Princess?"

Eve sighed. "Yes. I can't make him stop it. Anything I want, but that."

Parker smiled, his eyes warming. "Your father's an interesting man. A hard man with a very soft core."

Fiona and David came back to the table, holding hands. "I'm going to have to take this poor excuse of a man home," said Fiona. "So we'll say good-night now."

Parker looked at Eve. "Shall we go too?"

She nodded. "Four hours of steel band is probably enough!"

They drove back through the warm night, the breeze from the dark ocean blowing through the open Moke, feathering her skin, lifting her hair away from her face. It was nice not to be driving herself for a change, to be able to just sit back and enjoy the ride. It was nice to be sitting here next to Parker. No, not nice. It was another feeling—less placid and more disturbing. She was aware of a sense of fearful excitement. She knew the feeling, knew the name for it.

I'm in love, she thought. No, not just in love. I love him. I've always loved him. Acknowledging the truth made her heart suddenly beat faster.

"How about another drink, or a cup of coffee?" Parker suggested as they arrived back at the Plantation.

Apparently he wasn't ready to call it a night. Eve wasn't either. She didn't feel tired in the least.

She nodded. "I'd like that."

"Let's see what we can find."

Several people were still in the bar, an airy outdoor room off the lower floor terrace of the great house. Someone was playing the piano, some cool jazz with a Caribbean flavor to it. They found a table and sat down.

"Would you like a drink?" asked Parker.

She shook her head. "I'd rather have a cappuccino." She wasn't sure why she felt uneasy. She hadn't been alone with him like this, without anger, without feeling she had to defend herself against his insinuations.

She began to talk about Joshua, which was easy. Parker liked talking about his son.

"You enjoy being a father, don't you?" she asked, and he looked up, surprised.

"Yes."

"Where does Joshua stay when you're away on business?"

"With his grandparents—they live very close. He also goes there after school, until I come home from work. I have an excellent housekeeper, but his grandmother enjoys having him, and she takes him to his soccer practices after school."

She looked at the flowers on the table, absently touching the velvety petals. "You have a good relationship with Pamela's family, don't you?" she asked, feeling awkward asking the question, but still wanting to know.

"Yes—I always did. And since they're Joshua's family, I had no intention of taking him away from them when he came to live with me. Besides, I couldn't have done without them."

The waiter brought their coffee, and Eve looked down at the foamy milk sprinkled with chocolate. "Why didn't you and Pamela get married?" she asked.

He gave her a searching look. "Why are we talking about Pamela?"

She shrugged. "It came up. I guess I'm just plain vulgarly curious." She managed a half smile. She hadn't been curious before. She hadn't really wanted to know, but now she did.

He frowned. "Pamela and I were too much alike. We were good friends, but we didn't stimulate each other. Our relationship just sort of stagnated." He shrugged lightly. "We weren't the right combination of personalities to make a marriage work."

And we were? Eve wanted to ask. In retrospect it didn't make much sense. She wished desperately that she knew what he had seen in her five years ago, why he had loved her and wanted to spend the rest of his life with her, but this wasn't the time to ask.

"Why didn't Pamela tell you about Joshua?" she asked instead. She couldn't help but feel that a man had the right to know if he was a father.

His mouth quirked. "Because she knew me very well. She knew I would have insisted we get married, and she also knew it was the wrong thing. We wouldn't have been happy in the long run." He took a drink from his coffee, then put the cup back on its saucer. He leaned his arms on the table. "Tell me about you. Tell me about your accident and what happened afterward. Or would you rather not?"

"I don't mind." He didn't want to talk about Pamela any more, obviously, but it seemed to her that it wasn't because it made him uncomfortable. The tone of his voice had simply indicated that she was a part of his life that was long over. And she, Eve, was not.

So she told him about the accident and the operations and the years of therapy and her studies. Parker listened intently, smiling when she finished.

"You're so damn stubborn," he said, and there was admiration in his voice.

"I had to be, or I'd be spending my life with crutches or sitting in a wheelchair."

"You didn't have to go back to university."

"Oh, but I did! I had to, just to stay sane."

He laughed. "And I suppose you just had to come to this tiny island and go to work in an orphanage."

Eve gave him a cheery smile. "Right—I had to. Kismet, destiny, whatever you want to call it." She sipped the cappuccino slowly. Was it destiny that the two of them were on this island together now? Parker had commented on the coincidence some time ago. Maybe it's fate, he'd said. There was an odd look in his eyes now, and she wondered if he was thinking the same thing. She put the cup down, lowering her gaze.

They lingered over their coffee and afterward they walked along the moon-silvered path leading to the cottages. Crickets filled the air with their shrill chirping. At the turnoff to his own cottage, he stopped walking and took her hand.

The tension seemed suddenly electric. She was very aware of standing there so close to him in the warm, tropical night, aware of his body, his eyes looking at her. She felt the vibrations between them. The air was still and breathless as if even nature was waiting.

"Come with me," Parker said softly. It wasn't really a command, but neither was it a question. She went with him without a word. In the dark, the lush tropical foliage all around and the tall palms above made for an almost primeval atmosphere—mysterious, romantic, filled with small sounds and the sweet fragrance of jasmine. The Garden of Eden at night, she thought, and smiled. His hand was warm and strong, spreading its warmth all through her. It all seemed too beautiful to be real, as if she was merely dreaming it, her head all lightness and longing.

They moved inside and he let go of her hand, turning to the stereo equipment hidden in a rattan cabinet. He found a tape and inserted it, soft music rippling gently through the air. He came back to where she was standing and took both her hands, meeting her eyes.

"You know what I wanted to do all evening?" His voice was soft, seductive.

Her mouth went dry. She shook her head.

"I wanted to dance with you."

Her heart seemed to turn over. It was what she had wanted too. "I can't," she said, her voice low.

"But you can stand and I can hold you."

"Yes."

Parker slipped his arms around her and she lifted her own and put them around his neck. He lowered his head to touch hers. They swayed gently, a sensual moving, cheek to cheek. Images flashed in her mind of all the times they had been in each other's arms, dancing. How she had loved it then, doing all the modern dances as well as the classics—waltzes, tango, samba, jive. She remembered swinging, skirts swirling, feeling the exhilaration as her body moved to the rhythms of the music, laughing delightedly into Parker's smiling eyes. He was a good dancer, and it had surprised her a little.

The music swirled around her, luring her senses. Her earlier unease slowly faded away, to be replaced by a restless stirring in her blood. She rested her head in the hollow of his neck, her mouth against his warm skin, letting the music fill her, sweep all thoughts away. Her body was alive, every nerve end tingling with rich, vibrant sensations.

His hand began to stroke her back, her waist, her hip with just enough pressure that she could feel his restraint. He was holding her close, so close she seemed to feel every inch of his body against her own, felt as if there was nothing separating them now, no clothes, no time, no sadness, as if the music had woven a spell of magic around them, a sphere of consciousness where nothing but the moment was real.

This was real. She was in Parker's arms and it was the only place she ever wanted to be. She felt overwhelmed with emotion, a mixture of such power and intensity that tears came to her eyes.

His mouth trailed a sensuous path from her temple to her forehead, her eyes. He drew back slightly.

"You're crying," he said, his voice low and husky. "Oh, Eve, I'm sorry. I shouldn't have..."

She shook her head. "It's not that...it's just..." It's just that it feels so good to be held by you, it's because I still love you and it's overwhelming me. But she wasn't sure it would be the right thing to say.

"It's just what?" he asked.

"It just feels so good to have you hold me," she said huskily, not going on to say the rest.

"It feels good to hold you." He began to kiss her again, a kiss full of love and desire, a kiss that spoke a thousand words that had no name.

When the music stopped, he didn't release her immediately. "Come with me," he said again, his mouth close to her ear, and took her hand and led her into his bedroom. Moonlight spilled over the big bed, and he gave her an amused little smile. "Perfect," he said softly.

They undressed each other with trembling hands, touching with impatient longing. His mouth was warm on her skin, kissing her into sweet dizziness, filling her with delicious yearning. Then he lifted her up into his arms and put her down on the bed. He lay down next to her, leaning on one elbow and looking down at her, smiling. With his free hand he trailed tantalizing circles on her right breast. "This is the other thing I wanted," he said. "Having you in my bed."

Eve put her hand on his hair-roughened chest, feeling his heartbeat under her palm. "You're too far away." She wanted him closer. She wanted to feel his body, alive and aroused, against her own.

"I like looking at you." His dark eyes slid over her, his gaze like a caress. Her body quivered under his regard. The moonlight washed over his back and shoulders. He was beautiful, his dark skin glowing, his black hair gleaming in the silver light. Warmth flooded through her. She put her arms around his neck and drew him to her.

"I like feeling you against me," she whispered.

She felt him smile against her mouth. "I do like that too. You feel . . . soft, lovely. I want to touch you, taste you . . ."

Her mouth opened under his, his tongue meeting hers in a dance of sensual delight, teasing, touching, withdrawing.

She hadn't known she would ever want him so much, with so much deep, aching need, a great hunger flowing from her very soul. She moaned softly, stirring against him, tangling her fingers into the thickness of his hair.

Magic, she thought dizzily, this was truly magic. Every inch of her was alive, pulsing with exquisite sensation. She ran her hands over his body, stroking smooth skin and strong muscles, feeling angles and forms so different from her own. He tasted and smelled and felt familiar, yet it was all excitingly new and intoxicating. She loved him, she loved his body, she loved making love with him. She loved the way he made her feel.

He groaned softly. "Eve," he whispered. "Eve..."

Time fell away and she floated, weightless, as she reveled in the feel of his warm, throbbing body, the whispered words she did not really understand. His usual control had given way to a stormy desire and his mouth and hands swept her away into intolerable tension. She felt wild and wanton, all restraint gone, just wanting, yearning, her body aflame.

He lifted away slightly and looked at her, his eyes dark. Tender words...soft moans...they melded together, trembling, taking together the wild, breathless flight into the wondrous heights of passion where stars exploded in darkness. They clung together, shattered by the force, taking in convulsive breaths. She felt the wetness of tears on her cheeks.

Slowly they floated down into peaceful tranquillity, lying wordlessly in each other's arms. Eve's body felt heavy, sated. Parker was stroking her hair, her face, and she felt herself drifting into drowsy slumber, still holding on. Holding on, because she never again wanted to let him go.

She awoke in the morning with a delicious sense of well-being, but as consciousness returned fully she realized that she was alone in bed and Parker was gone. She took a towel from the bathroom, wrapped it around herself sarong-style, and went in search of him. Maybe he was out on the terrace waiting for her. He wasn't there. He wasn't anywhere else in the cottage either, and she felt her spirits sink with a crash. There was a vacuum coffeepot on the table and some fruit. A note leaned against the pot. "Went to the airport to pick Potter up. See you later. Parker." Eve crumpled the paper and threw it across the room in frustration. It was a stupid little note, factual, businesslike. Well, that was the way he was.

She sighed. Grow up, she told herself. The man had to leave. It's not his fault.

She went back to her own cottage, showered and went in search of breakfast. She didn't feel like being alone, so she walked over to the breakfast terrace at the great house. The Hollywood screenwriters were there among the few guests. They waved her over and invited her to join them.

"Do you know anything about that little church in Ginger Bay? The Ark of Love Catholic Church?" Elsa wanted to know. They were brainstorming a new idea for a movie, she said vaguely, and the little church, for some reason, interested them.

Eve took a sweet roll and buttered it. "It's Sunday. Go to Mass, see the place in action."

They seemed to think this an interesting idea. "Do you know the priest?" asked John.

Eve nodded. "I know Father Matthias. He comes to the orphanage to visit the children." She offered to go with them and introduce them to him.

She had no particular plans for this day and going to church on a Sunday morning seemed a reasonable sort of thing to do. She had spent all her childhood Sunday mornings in church with her father and grandmother, albeit a Presbyterian church and not a Catholic one.

People looked at them curiously as they entered the church. The three of them sat down behind Emmaline, who owned the grocery store in the village. Emmaline wore a straw hat with a flower arrangement all around, the color matching her prim blue belted dress. Eve tapped her on the shoulder and said hello, and Emmaline turned and smiled, pleased to see her. She smelled of sandalwood soap. Her four daughters were sitting quietly next to her, dressed in beautifully ironed cotton dresses with puffed sleeves and white collars, their hair neatly braided and adorned with colorful bows and clips. Emmaline's husband was not there. He was employed at the Plantation and probably on duty today.

Elsa leaned closer to Eve. "My, God, that hat!" she whispered. "I love it!"

After Mass, they lingered with the other parishioners, who stayed to chat and pass on the latest news. Eve introduced Elsa and John to Father Matthias, who was delighted to see them. He was even more delighted to see Eve. He smiled at her, clasping her hand between his. "You look very well today," he told her, eyes twinkling. "Very well indeed, Miss Eve."

She hadn't really blushed in years, and she didn't now, but she came precariously close.

She came back home to find a note from Parker on the terrace table. If she wasn't busy, would she join him for tea by the pool at four?

So he'd come back to look for her after he'd picked up the lawyer. Had he been disappointed to find her gone?

Eve glanced at her watch. She'd have a light lunch, write a letter to Sophie and read her book. Suddenly she couldn't wait for the time to pass.

When she arrived at the pool at four, Parker was in the water, swimming. He lifted his arm and gestured to one of the tables hidden in a green corner at the far end of the pool. It was already set with a blue and white floral tablecloth, and a beautiful set of china tea dishes in a white and blue pattern. A platter of finger sandwiches, fruit tarts and scones, all artfully arranged, lay in wait to tempt the weak. The picture was completed with a small bouquet of tiny white orchids. Eve smiled and sat down at the table. At the Plantation they knew how to do things right.

Parker lifted himself out of the pool and rubbed himself dry with a towel. "Glad you could make it," he said.

Eve looked around. "Where's Joshua? I thought he was coming back today."

Parker gave a crooked smile. "He sent a message. He needs another night to practice sleeping in the hammock, to get the hang of it, he said. Also he wants to buy three so he can take them home, hang them in the yard and have his friends over to sleep in them." He rolled his eyes.

Eve laughed. "I wish you luck with that project."

He pulled a shirt over his head and raked his fingers through his hair. "Am I presentable for tea?"

"Probably not at Buckingham Palace, but here you are. Where's your lawyer friend?"

Parker sat down at the table and leaned back, stretching out long legs. "I've stashed him in his room and he's reading the business plan and working on documents.'' He grinned. ''Don't worry about him; he's having a ball.'' He rubbed his shoulder and sighed. ''Two more weeks. I'll miss this place.''

Eve smiled. ''If you reserve now, they'll have a place for you next year, if you're lucky.''

''I only reserved a month in advance this time.''

''There must have been a cancellation.'' She watched him rubbing his shoulder. She'd seen him do it several other times too. ''What's the matter with your shoulder?'' she asked.

He shrugged. ''I hurt it last year, playing tennis. It never really got all the way better.''

''It hurts when you swim?''

''Yes, and when I play tennis.''

She asked him some more questions. How long had this been going on? Had he seen a doctor? She made him move his shoulder in various ways.

''I think you've got adhesions between the fascia and the muscle,'' she told him. ''It's not unusual if you've had an injury.''

''Sounds lovely. What the hell does that mean?''

She explained it to him. ''I can give you some myofascial release, if you want to. It should help.''

''How?''

''I can deep-massage your shoulder but it won't feel good,'' she warned.

Parker raised his eyebrows. ''Isn't massage supposed to feel good?''

''This isn't your run-of-the-mill massage. What I'll be doing is working deeply, loosening the fascia from the muscle. It'll hurt.''

''It hurts already,'' he said dryly. ''Where's the relief come in?''

''Not until later. You...''

His mouth curved in a smile, his eyes gleaming suggestively.

"Oh, for Pete's sake, stop leering!" She bit her lip, trying not to laugh. "You may not feel it right away. I may have to work on it a couple of times before it feels much better."

"I'd appreciate it if you'd give it a try." His face was smooth again. "But let's have tea first."

Eve picked up the pretty pot and poured them each a cup. "You used not to drink tea," she said, repeating what he'd said to her a while back.

"When in Rome..." he smiled. "It fits this place— the life-style, the surroundings, the ambience."

"When you're back in Philly, next time you have a board meeting, just have a catered tea..." She stopped and laughed, picturing the scene in the stuffy paneled boardroom with the members in their dark suits sipping tea from delicately flowered china cups and eating cucumber sandwiches.

He gave her a long, dark look. "Somehow I don't think it will fit."

"Oh, but you have to do this right," she said, laughing. "Listen..."

Parker shook his head and rolled his eyes. "You and your crazy ideas."

The words seemed to hang in the air between them and the smile suddenly faded from his face. Eve swallowed, feeling an odd sense of being thrown back in time. "You and your crazy ideas." He'd said that to her a hundred times, smiling, laughing. "What would I do without you? Life would be so boring."

She glanced away, at the water sparkling in the sun. One of the peacocks came strutting out of the bushes, looked around haughtily and strutted right back into the greenery as if the pool scene had offended him.

"Arrogant beasts," Parker said casually.

"Yes." She stirred a little sugar into her tea and took one of the tarts. "How long is this Potter character going to be here?"

"He's leaving at the end of the week." Parker took a sandwich off the tray. "Joshua's going back with him." School would start soon, Parker explained, and Joshua's grandmother would take him shopping for clothes and supplies.

After tea, they went back to Parker's cottage so that Eve could work on his shoulder. She had him take off his shirt and told him to sit down.

"Relax," she said, resting her hand on his shoulder. His skin felt smooth and warm.

"Sure," he said. "I always do before I get tortured."

"Men are such babies!"

"Watch it," he said darkly, and she laughed.

She worked on his shoulder, watching his face. He wasn't enjoying it, that was clear.

"You're hurting me," he complained.

"I know."

"You get a kick out of that, don't you?"

Eve made a face. "Yes. I like hurting people, especially people like you."

"What's that supposed to mean?"

"I don't know. I'm just making polite conversation."

He laughed, then groaned. "Your hands are lethal weapons, woman!"

She smiled at him sweetly. "You just remember that."

After a few more minutes she let her hands fall away. "That'll do for now," she announced.

"They do it better in Bangkok."

She raised one eyebrow. "They do what better in Bangkok?"

"Massages."

"I didn't give you a massage. I gave you physiotherapy. If you want a massage, call the desk. We have a masseuse on the staff. She's very good too."

Parker took her hand and pulled her onto his knees. "I don't want a strange woman fooling around with my body," he whispered in her ear. His hands stroked her hair, slowly, sensuously.

"Why not?" she whispered back. "It would feel good."

"Not as good as something else I can think of." His mouth brushed her lips, teasing, tantalizing.

"What's that?"

"Do I have to spell it out for you?"

"Yes," she murmured. "Spell it out for me."

CHAPTER NINE

PARKER began to unbutton her blouse, slowly, teasingly. Through the thin fabric Eve felt his touch on her breasts, as he no doubt intended. She felt her nipples tingle and harden. He smiled into her eyes and she sat very still, allowing the sensations to flow through her, warming at the look in his eyes. He slipped the blouse off her shoulders and down her arms, then unfastened her bra.

He cupped her breasts in his hands. They were white against the deep tan of his big hands. "How does this feel?" he asked.

"Nice," she said, reaching up to trail her fingers through his hair. He bent his head and kissed her breasts. She felt the heat of his mouth, the tingling sensation shooting tiny stars of heat all through her. She slid her hands down his bare back and closed her eyes, letting out a small sigh.

"I want you," he whispered, lifting his head and seeking her mouth in a long, lingering kiss, while his hands did terribly seductive things that made her wriggle on his lap. "Sit still, woman," he groaned.

"I can't! You..."

He silenced her with his mouth, his hands continuing his wanderings, and she struggled helplessly. She began to laugh, breaking the kiss. He gave her a smoldering look, pushed her off his knees and propelled her into the bedroom where he dropped her unceremoniously on the bed.

"I'll teach you to laugh at me," he said darkly, lying down on top of her, holding her captive.

"Please," she said, grinning up at him.

There was more laughter, which later stilled in the trembling passion of their damp bodies. Lying on the tangled bed, arms, and legs and bodies entwined, they made love until the sun left the sky and draped the room in dark shadows.

Eve lay drowsily in his arms, her mouth against the warmth of his neck, her hand on his chest. She felt the steady beating of his heart, calm now, and she wished she could stay like this forever, to have the feeling last and last.

Some time later, Parker rolled over and looked at the bedside clock. He groaned. "I'm having dinner with Potter in half an hour. Come with me, please?"

"Why? You're just going to be talking business."

He put his mouth on her breast and gave her tiny little kisses. "I don't want you out of my sight. I want to make sure your red-bearded pirate-doctor doesn't slip ashore and take off with you."

"Maybe we have business to discuss," she said lightly, pressing down a sudden uneasiness.

Parker lifted his head. "Is there anything between you two?"

She tensed. "Yes," she said curtly. "St. Mary's, a bunch of kids and a lot of friendship." What did he think? That she was having an affair with Nick and sleeping with him at the same time? She sat up and moved away from him, feeling suddenly cold and depressed. How could he even think that? Well, why not? He hadn't seen her in five years. How could he really know anything about her?

His arm pulled her back down. "I'm sorry," he said. "I didn't mean to insinuate..."

"Well, you did."

He looked at her silently, his eyes holding hers. "I've seen the two of you together a couple of times. You seem very…comfortable together. I couldn't help but wonder about your relationship. I'm sorry, I didn't mean to offend you, Eve."

He hadn't meant to, she knew that. Yet his question had made it clear how much unknown territory still lay between them. She sighed and shrugged. "Let's forget it. You'd better get going or you'll be late for your dinner with Mr. Potter."

"Potter be damned," he muttered, drawing her close against his warm, naked body, and kissing her deeply. Eve felt her anger melting. It was hard to resist him. She didn't want anger between them. She wanted love and understanding. She wondered how long it would take.

"Forgive me?" Parker whispered against her mouth.

"Yes," she whispered back.

"Will you join us for dinner?"

"If you really want me to."

"I really want you to."

Miles Potter was a colorless little man with thin, sandy hair and watery blue eyes. When he talked, his voice was as monotonous as his appearance was colorless. He was not interested in the island, the beach, or the people. His only passion was for law, although passion wasn't a word one would associate with this bland little man. As he and Parker were talking shop, Eve was imagining him kissing a woman, and couldn't. Then she started imagining Parker kissing her, and could, very easily.

She watched the man eat his dinner and wanted to scream. He ate slowly, carefully, as if he expected razor blades hiding in every morsel. All Eve could think of was getting it over with. He did eventually excuse himself, declining dessert, and disappeared to go back to his suite of rooms at the main Plantation building to go back to work.

Parker took her hand. "Thank you for joining us for dinner."

She grimaced. "Where did you find him? He must be the most boring person in the world!"

"He's a brilliant lawyer."

"I bet he doesn't have much of a love life," Eve said nastily. Being bored got the worst out of her. She also conveniently forgot that until very recently, she'd not had much of a love life herself.

Parker grinned. "Now, now! Shame on you. He's married and has three children."

"You're kidding!"

"No. Still waters and all that. How about some dessert?"

"Definitely. The most sinful there is."

Later they walked to the beach in the dark, holding hands, and sat down in the powdery sand. Eve's dress was a bright colored cotton that could stand up to a little dry sand. Parker wound his arms around her and held her close, and for a while they sat silently, not moving. Eve felt her body stir into life in the sensuous intimacy of the embrace. It came so easily, so naturally. She sighed and huddled closer against him. The murmur of the waves seduced her, weaving a web of romance and mystery. It was dark, a soft, velvety darkness with only the silver moon glimmering on the tranquil sea.

Parker turned his head, searching for her mouth, and kissed her. She reveled in the feel of his firm, warm mouth, gave herself up to its yearning intensity with heady delight. She gave a soft moan of protest when he broke away. He gave a soft, amused laugh.

"That's what I wanted to do all evening while I watched you being so utterly civilized at dinner."

"I was very well brought up," she whispered against his cheek. "My grandmother was a true Southern lady."

"Did she teach you to play footsie under the table?"

"I'm the creative type. I came up with that myself."

He smiled. "Tell me something. You've been here on this tiny island for more than a year. Why aren't you bored to tears? It's a beautiful place, but there isn't much to do." He trailed his hands through her hair with gentle, sensuous movements, tugging gently at her curls. "I keep asking myself why you're here, why you're working here with these kids."

She glanced up at the sky, seeing the millions of stars, the silver crescent of the moon. "I suppose it's because I feel...needed." She met his eyes, giving a self-conscious smile. "I never felt needed before."

Parker gave her an incredulous look.

She frowned. "What's so strange about that? It's important to feel needed. I *like* feeling needed."

He looked at her in silence, an odd expression on his face, and she felt a stirring of apprehension.

"What's wrong?" she whispered.

"You've never felt needed before?"

Eve shook her head. "No, not in any real, meaningful sense."

He closed his eyes briefly. "I needed you, Eve." His voice was low and pained.

She stared at him, her heart beating in uneasy rhythm. "Because of Joshua?"

He shook his head. "Not just because of Joshua. I needed you long before that. I *always* needed you."

"Oh." It was a whisper. She didn't know what to think, what to say. She felt overwhelmed.

"Eve? Is that such a surprise? Didn't you *know*?"

She shook her head. "I...I don't understand." Her right hand dug into the sand.

"What don't you understand?"

"You don't seem like somebody who needs anybody," she said slowly. "I mean...you're confident and strong and self-reliant...and...I just never thought of you as *needing* me."

His face was full of dark shadows. "How did you think of me, then? Why did you think I wanted to marry you?"

She swallowed. "You said you loved me. You wanted me."

"Why do you think I loved you?"

She felt a piercing pain. Tears burned behind her eyes. It was the question she had asked herself a hundred times. And a hundred times she had found no answer. Her hands clenched into fists in her lap, sand gritty between her fingers. "I don't know." Her voice sounded agonized in her own ears. Tears clouded her eyes, blurring everything. *"I don't know!"*

"I loved you and I needed you," Parker said quietly. "But you don't know why?"

"No!" There was a note of hysteria in her voice. "How could you possibly love me, then? I was selfish, spoiled rotten—I only thought of myself. I always got what I wanted. I had everything and didn't think anything of it. I was so damned *shallow*! How could you possibly love me? How could you possibly *need* me?"

His arm tightened around her shoulder and he smiled. "It wasn't hard, you know."

She wiped at her eyes and swallowed. "I can't imagine it."

"Eve, you were bubbly, happy, joyful, all the things I was not. You made me laugh, you made me feel alive.

You were the missing piece in my life. Oh, Eve," he said softly, "how could you not know?"

"I don't know," she whispered.

"At the time, why did you think I loved you? Because you were beautiful, rich?"

She took in an unsteady breath. "Maybe. I took it for granted. Everybody thought I was wonderful, you know. It never occurred to me to think I wasn't lovable. I was so damned arrogant and self-centered. I was sure any man would love me if only I'd be good enough to give him the chance."

He laughed. "Oh, Eve!"

"I was horrible," she insisted.

"No, you weren't. You were wonderful. You were funny. You made me laugh." She felt his mouth on her temple. "You're still funny," he whispered. "You still make me laugh." He kissed her again, and she thought of the laughter they had shared only hours before, the love they had made, and new desire sprang up inside her, driving all thoughts from her head. There was magic in his mouth and hands, magic in the night around them.

"Make love to me," she whispered.

In the morning he was gone. She stared up at the high, peaked ceiling of her bedroom, feeling disappointment seep through her every cell. It had been so good, so right. Why couldn't he have stayed?

She climbed out of bed, her limbs heavy. She wasn't sure why she felt a vague uneasiness. Everything had been fine, hadn't it? They'd fallen alseep, holding each other. She glanced around the bedroom. Parker's clothes were gone. There was nothing to indicate that he'd been there.

Eve showered and dressed. She couldn't expect one delirious weekend to bridge the emptiness of five years, could she? It would take time.

Later in the afternoon, soon after she came back from St. Mary's, Parker appeared at her cottage, several sheets of paper in hand. His jaw was hard, rigid, his dark eyes angry.

"Look at this," he said, his voice cold and uncontrolled. He tossed the papers on the table in front of her. "I thought you might find this interesting."

She picked up the papers and glanced at them, not comprehending. They were business documents, and she couldn't imagine what she was meant to find interesting about them. They had nothing to do with her. "What's this about?" she queried. "What am I looking for?"

"Ever heard of Telenology Inc.?"

She shook her head. "No." His anger frightened her.

"It's the company wanting to go into partnership with us on this data-processing project." He gave her a narrow-eyed look. "You're sure you've never heard of that name?"

Her body tensed. "No. Should I have?"

He shrugged. "Not necessarily, I suppose. I just found out from Potter that it's one of the companies in the Ashwell Group."

"Oh," she said, trying madly to figure out what was the meaning of all this.

His eyes held hers. "Add it all up, Eve, and what do you get?"

She threw the papers back on the table, losing her patience. "Add what all up?"

"You mean to say you know nothing about one of your father's companies wanting to go into partnership with mine?"

"No! I don't keep up with all his dealings! I have nothing to do with them! Will you stop being mysterious, for heaven's sake? Why are you mad at me? What am I supposed to understand?"

Parker sighed and ran his hand through his hair. "Never mind. You don't know all the details and I'll spare you the explanation. Suffice it to say that I believe I'm not on St. Barlow by sheer coincidence. I'm certain your father orchestrated this crafty little setup."

She felt her heart sink. "Oh, damn," she muttered. She stared at him. "I had nothing to do with this. I don't know why..."

His eyes bored into hers. "Are you sure?"

"Yes, I'm sure!" She glared at him. "I don't know anything about this!" Her voice shook. "And if you want to be mad at somebody, be mad at my father, not me!"

Parker cursed under his breath, turning his back on her. This gesture of dismissal infuriated her. "Look at me! Do you think I *asked* my father to get you out to St. Barlow?"

He turned to face her. "No," he said slowly. "No, I don't think so. Thinking of your behavior and reactions when I arrived, it wouldn't make sense."

"Thank you," Eve said coldly.

"Damn that man!" he muttered fiercely. His hands were balled into fists, the knuckles white.

She wondered what he was thinking, if he was angry he'd been set up, if he was sorry he'd ever set foot on the island.

"Are you sorry you came?" she asked, feeling fear flow through her like ice water.

He sighed heavily, pacing the room. "I'm not sorry I met you again, if that's what you mean. I'm just damn furious to find I've been manipulated."

Ah, his pride had taken a beating. Well, she could understand his feelings. It must be some blow to his ego to discover he had been outmaneuvered by her father. She bit her lip. It was almost funny.

He scrutinized her face, eyes narrowed. "What are you laughing at?" he asked.

"I'm not laughing." It was hard to keep her face straight. It was such sweet relief to know he wasn't sorry he'd met her again. He was angry with her father. She didn't mind that. Her father could take care of himself.

"Oh, yes, you are," he said softly, coming toward her. He put his hands on her shoulders, looking into her eyes with dark menace. It didn't quite hide the sudden glimmer of humor that sprang up behind it. "Why are you laughing?"

Eve did laugh then. "I'm sorry," she said. "I don't mean to be laughing, truly, but you know, no real harm is done. It's just your pride that's bruised a little bit. But you're a big man and you can take it," she said soothingly. "You're brave and strong..."

Parker silenced her with a fierce kiss, at least it was intended to be a fierce kiss. It didn't work very well because she was laughing. He looked at her darkly.

"You think this is funny, don't you?"

"Only a tiny little bit," she said gravely, trying hard to keep her face straight.

He let go of her and stepped back. "It's a good thing I like your father or I'd put a price on his head. Have you spoken to him lately?"

"He calls me all the time," Eve told him.

"Has he mentioned me?"

"Yes."

"And what have you told him?"

"Mostly that you're hard at work and that he should mind his own business."

"He should," he said bluntly. "Do you let him run your life for you?"

She gave him a despairing look. "Would I be here if I did?"

Parker chuckled. "No, I imagine not." He moved to the table and picked up the papers. For a moment he looked at them pensively. "I was ready for murder when I figured out what had happened." He glanced up. "What did you do to calm me down?"

Eve smiled. "Magic."

His eyes held hers for a long moment. Then he came over and wrapped his arms around her. "Maybe you're right," he said softly. He kissed her quickly, then moved out onto the terrace and was gone.

Her father called that evening. He seemed to be calling more and more, and she was beginning to understand why. He was worried about what was really going on between her and Parker.

"You did a good job on Parker, didn't you?" she said abruptly.

"What do you mean?"

"Don't pretend ignorance, Dad, you know what I mean. You manipulated him. He isn't too happy about it."

"I had to do something."

"You're not supposed to play God with other people's lives, Dad! And why did you have to do something?"

"For God's sake, Eve!" he thundered, suddenly losing his temper. "You've buried yourself on that damned rock and you refuse to come back home! I want you happy! I want you married! I want grandchildren, come to that!"

"And you don't think I can find myself a husband?"

"The point is not whether you can or not. It's whether you are—and you're not! Five years since...well, not counting that loser Harrington. Five years and nothing, Princess! I'm not going to sit here and do nothing."

Eve could understand that. He was a man of action. Sitting back and waiting for things to happen was not his style. Under the circumstances, it was a miracle this hadn't happened sooner.

"But why Parker?" she asked. "Why did you have to dig him up out of the past?"

He sighed. "Eve, he's the only one you ever loved, the only man worth anything. I should never have called off that wedding. I should have talked some sense into you, instead of giving in to you."

"You aren't responsible for my mistakes."

"I was responsible for indulging you instead of teaching you responsibility!" His voice was sharp. "I've not done right by you, Eve, not by a long shot."

She felt a lump in her throat. "Oh, Dad! How can you say that? You've always been there for me. You've always loved me."

"I've made some serious mistakes." He sounded weary, and her heart ached for him.

"We all make mistakes! And I want you to stop feeling guilty, you hear? I'm fine, I'm happy. I'm doing what I want to be doing." She paused. "I can take care of myself, Dad."

After she had hung up, Eve sat for a long time staring out the window at the magnificent display of sky and sea and sand and palms, seeing amid the glorious greens and blues her father's face. He held himself responsible for her mistakes. He'd tried to make things right, fix what was broken. How could she possibly be angry with him?

*　　*　　*

There was another going-away party at St. Mary's the next day, this time for Tobias. More cake, more tears. The mother promised the nuns she'd send pictures. She was a warm, smiling woman with laughing eyes and an unmistakable sense of humor. She would need it in the time to come to help Tobias through his foot surgery.

On her way home from the orphanage, Eve noticed Father Matthias in front of the church with a small group of people. There were two local women with belted dresses and hats with flowers. One of them was holding a camera and was taking a picture of a young white couple. The girl had on a short white dress, and a crown of white flowers in her hair. The man was dressed in white cotton pants and a flowered shirt. The Hollywood screenwriters. So that was why they'd been so interested in the church! Eve grinned, tempted to turn the car and go back to the church, but decided not to. Obviously they'd wanted to do this in secrecy or they would have told her the truth rather than that tale about a movie script they were writing.

Eve drove on, gripped by sudden envy. She pushed it out of her head and concentrated on the road ahead of her.

She didn't see much of Parker in the next few days; he was busy with the humorless Miles Potter. At the end of the week the man would be gone. She couldn't help but look forward to it. She was filled with expectation, and every time she saw Parker, no matter how briefly, she felt her pulse leap.

Joshua had had a wonderful time in the village over the weekend and was full of stories. He had mixed feelings about returning to Philadelphia. He didn't like leaving his new friends, Kevin and Nelson. He most certainly didn't like having to travel home with the dour Mr. Potter. However, he was eager to see his old friends again and tell them about his adventures. Three hammocks had been purchased and packed for the trip back.

On Saturday, Eve went along to see Joshua and Miles Potter off at the airport. Fish was waiting for them, and for the Italian *contessa* who was leaving as well. He was flying them to St. Thomas where they would get connecting flights.

"Will you come and see us when you're in Philadelphia?" Joshua asked Eve when they said goodbye.

"I don't go to Philadelphia very often," she said evasively.

"But when you do," he persisted.

She smiled. "Sure. I'll call you and let you know."

"Okay." He gave a solemn little smile. Then, hesitating for a moment, he reached out to give her a hug. Eve felt tears prick behind her eyes as she held him close.

"Goodbye, Joshua," she whispered. "I'm glad I got to know you."

He stalked off toward the plane. Eve bit her lip, aware that Parker was watching her. She avoided meeting his gaze.

They waited until the plane had taken off, then got back into Parker's Moke, making small talk as they drove back to the Plantation. In two weeks, Parker was due to leave too. Two weeks wasn't a very long time. She didn't know what to hope for, what to expect.

"Do you have any plans for tonight?" he asked as they parked the car in the shade of a fig tree behind the estate house. He smiled. "I'm a free man again."

"What did you have in mind?" she asked lightly.

"A little dinner, a little wine, a moonlight swim. How would that be?"

"I'd like that."

*   *   *

And she did like it. It was an idyllic night. Parker had ordered an intimate dinner for two, served on the terrace of his cottage. There was candlelight and music and wine, and everything was just right. Later they were alone on the beach, and they swam and played in the water, naked, laughing like children in Paradise, until it was no longer a children's game and they went back to his cottage and made wonderful, passionate love.

The days that followed were like a dream. For a while Eve was filled with new hope, but slowly she came to the terrifying realization that something was wrong.

On the surface everything was fine. They shared a meal, went for a swim in the pool, they talked. They made love every night. Parker wanted her in his bed, there was no doubt about that, but outside it something was lacking.

Despite the nights they had spent together, she was aware of a certain reserve in him. She sensed in him a tension she did not know how to cope with. She wanted closeness, intimacy, something to bridge that barrier of five years, yet it wasn't happening.

She remembered how long it had taken to win him over after she had first met him. He was a difficult man to know. He didn't give of himself easily, and Eve sensed very clearly that he was holding back now. Sometimes she found him brooding and aloof, and fear clutched at her heart. She wished he would tell her what was on his mind, but he was silent, evasive.

They had never spoken about the day he had come to her father's house in Philadelphia and told her about Joshua, the day she had called off the wedding. That painful memory still seemed to hang like a dark cloud over their relationship. But in bed, while they were making love, all seemed forgotten.

Parker too had to come to terms with his own feelings, Eve was well aware of that. It was quite clear he was struggling with himself. Maybe the memories were still too painful. It would take time. She could only hope that he would get to know her the way she was now and forget that other girl who had hurt him so deeply.

The days passed and nothing changed. He did not tell her he loved her. He did not tell her he needed her. Six more days and he would leave. Eve began to feel increasingly unhappy and she didn't want to make love any more. She began to avoid him. It didn't take long for him to notice.

He came to her cottage one afternoon, just after she had come back from St. Mary's. The radio was on and she was absently listening to a weather report about a tropical storm brewing in the Atlantic east of Barbados. She looked up, startled to find Parker standing on the terrace. She hadn't heard him approach.

"I missed you last night," he said, entering the room and sitting down in one of the rattan chairs. "I didn't know you were gone."

Eve turned the radio off. "I was at Daniella's," she told him, feeling as if she were telling a lie. "We talked and it got late, so I stayed for the night." She took a sip from the passionfruit juice she had just poured herself. "She's leaving tomorrow, and I won't see her again for a year, probably." It was an excuse of sorts. Had she wanted to be with him last night, she could have easily come back.

His eyes met hers. "You're avoiding me, Eve," he said quietly.

She closed her eyes and covered her face with her hands. She wanted to make everything right, but she didn't know how. She felt powerless.

"Don't you want to sleep with me any more?" he asked.

She bit her lip. "I don't feel like it any more. It doesn't feel right."

"Why not?" His voice was tense.

Her throat closed. "Parker, you know why. Things aren't right between us."

There was a slight pause. "What isn't right, Eve?"

She stared at him, heart hammering. "You don't trust me. You don't love me." Her voice shook. "You haven't forgiven me."

She hadn't known she was going to say that, but now that she had, she knew it to be right. He didn't love her. He could not forgive her. It was as simple as that. And just as simple was the pain of that knowledge.

He stared at her, his face pale, not denying it, not saying a word, and she felt as if all her hopes and dreams came crashing down around her—crumbling like a gingerbread castle—sweet and pretty and hollow inside. Worthless.

CHAPTER TEN

THE silence stretched and the tightness in Eve's chest made it hard to breathe. She wanted to turn and run out, but that wouldn't solve anything. She could escape Parker, but she could not escape the problems. She swallowed hard, struggling desperately for composure. "I know something is going on between us, but...but the way it is it's difficult for me to handle it."

"I don't know what you expect of me," he said, his voice toneless. Eve knew that tone. I don't want to talk about it, it said.

"I think we need to talk," she said. She wasn't going to stop now. She wasn't going to let him stop her by that tone. "I think we need to talk about that time you came to tell me about Joshua. About the things I said."

Parker's jaw hardened. "There's no use in digging it all up. You said so yourself."

"Well, I was wrong." She met his eyes. They were dark and unreadable. "I think I understand your feelings, Parker. I would like you to try and understand mine. I know it's a lot to ask, but I'd like you to try."

Her legs were shaking and she sat down on the couch and took a deep breath. "I want you to know that I'll regret for the rest of my life what I've done to you."

He said nothing, his face expressionless, eyes withdrawn. Eve bit her lip. "A lot of things have happened to me in the last five years," she went on. She felt herself slump and straightened her shoulders. "When I think of myself five years ago, I don't recognize myself. When I think of what happened between us...I can't believe it happened. I know it happened, I just . . . I can't believe how shallow and selfish I was. It's like looking at a different person, someone I don't recognize.''

Parker was silent, not looking at her, staring broodingly into space.

She felt a sinking despair. ''There's no way to make up for what I did, no way to make it right—I know that. But I can't keep living in the past, and I can't go on feeling . . . feeling this terrible guilt.''

Still he said nothing, and a helpless anger took hold of her. She straightened and looked at him squarely. ''You've got to understand one thing, Parker! It's done! It's over, and nothing can change it! No matter how much I wish it never happened, it did! But I've got to be able to leave it behind. I'm no longer that person and I don't want to be! I'm me now, and I like myself, and I can't have the past keep eating away at my self-respect!'' She got up, her legs shaking. ''I'm not going to let it!'' She came to her feet, legs shaking, and walked into her bedroom, tears blinding her.

She'd forgiven herself, but what good would it do her if Parker could never forgive her?

She heard him leave a few minutes later. He hadn't followed her into the bedroom, and she was both relieved and disappointed. If only he would come and tell her everything was all right, that the past was the past, that nothing mattered except the present. If only he'd tell her he loved her . . .

The phone next to her bed began to ring. For a moment she contemplated letting it ring, but she'd never been able to do it and she wasn't now.

It was her father, calling from Sydney.

''Have you heard the weather report?'' he asked.

"Yes, I have, Dad." The tropical storm that had been brewing east of Barbados had turned into a full-fledged hurricane.

"Hurricanes aren't anything to fool around with. I want you to contact Fish and get off the island while you still can."

Eve sighed. "Oh, Dad! It's going to miss us—we're not in its path. We're just going to have some wind and rain."

"If the direction doesn't change," he said curtly. "Hurricanes are unpredictable, Princess. It won't take much of a change of direction to hit St. Barlow head-on. I want you off, Eve!"

"You're overreacting, Dad."

"You're my only child and I want you safe!" His voice indicated that he wanted no argument. He was the boss and she'd better do what she was told.

"I'll be safe enough here," she said, gritting her teeth. He was in Australia and there wasn't much he could do to force her from that distance. "The great house has survived hurricanes for centuries. I'll be careful." The great house had been built like a fort, with thick stone walls and heavy beams.

"I want you to watch the news tomorrow morning and listen to the reports from Miami. Don't pay attention to what the local news says, they don't know beans. If there's any chance it'll hit, get off right away, you hear me?"

Eve's hand tightened around the receiver. She told herself to be calm. "Of course I'll watch, Dad. I'm not a total idiot, I know what to do." She loved her father, but it was difficult not to lose her temper when he was doing his big manager routine and started ordering her around as if she were a brainless child.

"Guess what, Dad," she said, wanting to change the subject. "Darnell Robertson sent out an official request for a Peace Corps volunteer yesterday. He even gave me a copy."

Needless to say, her father was delighted. "I'll see what I can do to speed things up at this end," he assured her.

He probably could do a lot. Eve grimaced wryly as she replaced the receiver after she'd said goodbye. Once her father got into the action, she'd be back in Philadelphia before she knew it.

The next morning at seven she received a phone call from Fish, who was in Grenada.

"Your old man called me from Sydney," he told her, cool as a cucumber. "Wants me to come and rescue the maiden in distress." He spoke as if he got calls from Sydney on a daily basis.

Eve groaned. "I don't believe this! He's nuts!"

"Just afraid Ferdi's going to blow his little girl off the island," said Fish.

"Well, I'm not leaving! He's going to have to stop ordering me around!"

Fish chuckled. "You'd better be very sure. If you want me to come and get you, you'll have to tell me now. Later is too late, 'cause I'm not flying in any hurricane."

"It's not going to hit here! I just saw the report from Miami." The projections of the weathermen showed the hurricane's path east of the island, with the outer fringes sideswiping St. Barlow, causing strong winds and heavy rains. Nothing to joke about, surely, but nothing compared with a full hit.

"Well," he said easily, "you never know. So your mind is made up?"

"Yes! I'm staying right here."

"Too bad. He offered me a nice bonus."

"I'm not surprised."

He laughed. "Well, take care of yourself. Better start battening down the hatches. Ferdi should be coming by this afternoon."

She replaced the receiver. Outside everything was bright and sunny. A hummingbird fluttered over a yellow trumpet-shaped flower of the ginger thomas tree. A soft breeze gently rustled the palm fronds. Everything was very quiet, very peaceful.

For the first time, Eve felt a twinge of fear.

The storm hit in the late afternoon. The sky darkened suddenly, gray clouds wiping out the blue of the sky. Fearsome winds blew across the island from the Atlantic coast. Trees and palms bent and groaned. The noise of the wind was frightening. All the personnel at the Plantation had been working to get loose materials inside—furniture, loungers, potted plants. Hammocks were taken down, windows taped, shutters secured on all the cottages.

Inside the main building, most of the guests had gathered in an unusual show of congeniality and togetherness. Tea was served in the old dining hall, which was normally being used as a library. The tables from the courtyard had been set up, complete with flowers and candles. Guests, after all, should not be cheated out of their luxury, storm or no storm.

"I think they're wrong about it," someone said. "If it changes course at all, and I believe that's what's happening, Ferdinand is going to hit us head-on."

A direct hit by a hurricane would be a major disaster. The small chattel houses would be flattened, the crops destroyed, with people's livelihoods and income vanished. Everyone remembered Hurrican Hugo which had ravished Guadaloupe, the Virgin Islands and Puerto

Rico. Everyone remembered Hurrican Gilbert smashing into Jamaica.

Eve felt a growing fear. All those horror stories suddenly seemed more real with the storm howling around the building and tearing at the greenery outside. She wondered where Parker was. She hadn't seen him after he'd left her cottage the day before. She had lain awake for a long time, listening to the high-pitched squeals of the tree-frogs and the soft rushing of the waves, wishing he would come to her. But there'd been no footsteps in the dark, no knocking on her bedroom door.

After tea, she went back to her cottage. The wind was blowing hard, raindrops spattering on leaves. She felt restless, afraid, oddly excited. She wondered where the peacocks were, if someone had locked them up or if they were safer free. The sky looked dark and ominous, the air was eerily gray, washing the color out of the landscape.

She walked nervously around the cottage, looking up at the peaked ceiling. If that went, the whole cottage would be ruined. The windows had been taped earlier, the shutters had been secured tightly. Large shutters had been lowerd in front of the open end of the living room.

She was beginning to feel claustrophobic with the terrible noises coming from outside and no way to look out with everything closed up.

The phone rang. It was the Plantation manager.

"Eve, I'd feel better if you came here," he said. "We've been calling everybody to come to the great house until the storm is over, just to be safe."

"I'm all right here for now, Tom. I'll come over later."

"Please don't wait too long."

As she replaced the receiver, the electricity went off. A moment later it was back on as the resort's generator sprang into action. The island was in darkness. The

Government had cut off the electricity, as it had said it would, for safety measures. Once the storm grew any worse the power would go anyway, leaving tangles of live wires that killed people and started fires.

At St. Mary's that morning Eve had helped tape the windows, filled bottles and buckets of water, just in case, laughing because all the work almost surely would be unnecessary. Laughing too, to keep the children from being unduly worried. She hadn't been worried herself, not then, with the sun shining brightly and the breeze barely ruffling the palms. It was hard to believe that in this sunny paradise disaster could strike within hours.

Only a storm, she'd told everybody. That's what the Government says, that's what it says on TV. She had left St. Mary's early, watching the weather report from the National Hurricane Center in Miami again when she returned. Again it had shown the map, the course of the hurricane, predicting its path. It wasn't going to hit St. Barlow. It was going to pass it by with only some high winds and heavy rain.

She paced the room, hearing the wind howling. Hurricanes were unpredictable. They could change course unexpectedly. What if that happened?

Daniella and Marc had left, so she didn't have to worry about them. The house on its high perch might not survive the storm, but she wasn't concerned about that. Fiona's old estate house would be safe; it had a relatively sheltered location. She thought of St. Mary's. It was a much less secure building.

What if the eye of the hurricane hit the island? What about St. Mary's building? What about the children?

Her hands felt clammy and and she felt the nervous rhythm of her own heart. Something terrible was going to happen, she could feel it in her bones. She had to get the children out of St. Mary's before it was too late. The nuns would be nervous. Half the children couldn't even walk without help.

She took a deep breath. She'd need some help. No— she'd better do it by herself. If she tried to get somebody to help, they'd make her stay here. Nobody would go out now.

She pulled on jeans and sneakers and a T-shirt and tied her hair back. Her little Moke would be blown off the road and it didn't hold enough people. If she took one of the vans she could crowd them all in one run. She'd take them back to the Plantation.

She walked out into the rain. It was only five in the afternoon, but outside the darkness was complete. The wind tore at her clothes, but it wasn't too bad yet. She moved as quickly as she could, around the great house, past the cobblestoned courtyard, oddly bare and deserted with the tables and chairs gone. Leaves and twigs littered the wet cobblestones. She went into the servants' entrance. She knew where the keys were kept, prayed nobody would see her. They'd prevent her from going if they knew what she was up to. She prayed the vans had automatic transmission; she couldn't remember. A standard transmission was hell on her left leg, although she could manage it if she had to. If you had to, you could move mountains. She had the idea she'd do a lot of praying before the storm was past. She kept talking to herself as she moved inside, silently, found the keys and made it outside without having been detected.

Both vans had standard transmission. Her heart sank. Oh, please, please, she prayed, it's not fair. I can't do this!

She *had* to do this. She climbed inside one of the vans and checked the fuel gauge. She turned on the lights and started the engine, gritting her teeth as she pushed down on the clutch. Slowly she crawled out of the parking lot, onto the winding road that led out of the Plantation property to Old Sugar Mill Road. If anybody heard her leave now, it would be too late to stop her.

The van felt big and unwieldy. It took an effort to handle the clutch. After a year of driving nothing but her little toy car, it was not surprising. The windshield wipers could barely keep up with the rain, and as she moved slowly down the road she kept on praying as she peered into the gray, impenetrable curtain of rain. The wind tore at the car, but she managed to keep it under control.

It seemed to take an eternity before she finally reached the village. It seemed deserted and was in complete darkness, with only here and there a glimmer of light from a candle or gas lantern escaping through a crack in the wooden shutters. The people must be terrified, knowing their houses didn't stand a chance if the hurricane hit the island.

The hurricane is not going to hit, she told herself. Miami says so. Miami was thousands of miles away. Miami was safe. Miami could be wrong.

Just drive, she told herself. Keep your mind on your business. You're almost there now—less than a mile. Less than half a mile...a quarter of a mile...

In the grey wall of rain, her headlights caught something big and dark. Her heart in her throat, she put her foot on the brake. The car slipped dangerously, came to a stop inches away from a tree sprawling across the road.

"No," she whispered, "Please, no!" She climbed out, breathless for a moment as the wind whipped away her breath. It was a papaya tree, skinny, shallow-rooted, that lay like a barrier straight across the road. As trees went, it was not much of one, yet it might as well have been a mango tree or an avocado tree for all she could do about it. She couldn't move it. There was no one around to help.

Panic flooded through her, then she squashed it, feeling a sudden icy determination.

She'd simply leave the car by the side of the road, climb over this miserable excuse of a tree and walk the rest of the way. It wasn't that far. They'd just have to get the children out, walk them, carry them, whatever it took, back to the van. There was no choice.

She turned the car, clenching her teeth as she worked the clutch and left it just off the road. She began to walk to the orphanage. It took her fifteen minutes, yet it seemed an hour. She was breathless and soaked through by the time she stumbled up the path. The lights were on, thanks to the generator. They were all huddled in the center room, away from the windows. The nuns looked terrified. The children looked terrified. The house creaked, and the wind howled around the corners.

Eve didn't know how she managed it, but somehow she got them all stirred into action. The three grown-ups carried the smaller children. Two of the older children pushed strollers with two toddlers. Timothy said he could manage with his crutches.

They moved out into the rain, and the babies began to cry. Eve shone her flashlight on the bedraggled little group. It was the most pathetic procession she had ever seen. Oh, please, she thought, let me be doing the right thing. This house just isn't going to hold up.

They struggled through the darkness, the wind tearing at them, the noise thundering in their ears. Eve headed up the group with her flashlight, carrying a three-month-old baby. Thank God Tobias had been picked up by his adoptive parents—there would have been no way to carry four children. Leaves and twigs blew in her face. Strands of hair whipped across her eyes. Her left leg ached.

It took them half an hour to negotiate the stretch of road up to the fallen papaya tree. The road was littered with fallen branches and odds and ends of debris. One of the girls fell, scraping a knee and an arm. Everyone started crying.

"We have to be brave!" Eve shouted, trying to be heard above the wind. "We'll be safe soon."

They crawled over the papaya tree, then, drenched and crying, the children got into the van. Eve gave the baby to Sister Angelica, who put him on her other knee. Eve sank down into the driver's seat and closed the door, heaving a sigh of relief. She lowered her head on her arms resting on the steering wheel and tried to catch her breath. She had not counted on it being a job just getting the children into the van.

She lifted her head and smiled bravely at the children. "We're going to find a nice dry place for us to stay, okay? We'll have something to drink and something to eat and wait for the storm to pass."

She got no reaction. They were terrified beyond consolation.

She gritted her teeth and pushed in the clutch. She started the engine and drove slowly down the road, bumping over loose rocks, branches and clumps of mud and leaves. At least no one else was as insane as she, and the road was empty of traffic. She moved through the village, continuing on Old Sugar Mill Road toward the Plantation and safety.

The children grew quiet. Sister Angelica was sitting with her eyes closed, her lips moving in prayer as she clutched the two babies against her chest.

Hope was growing. If all went well, they'd be back at the Plantation in twenty minutes.

All did not go well.

Peering into the wet curtain of darkness, her shoulders and neck aching, Eve noticed another obstruction. She stopped the car, her heart pounding in panic. Oh, no, this wasn't fair! She'd tried, she'd tried! She needed a little help, just a little! Please keep the road clear, please, please...

This time it was not a puny papaya tree, but a massive heap of mud and rock, worked loose by the rain higher up the mountainside and slipped down on to the road. They couldn't move it, they couldn't go over or around it.

She got back in the car and slumped over the wheel. "I've got to think," she said out loud, forcing herself not to give in to panic. "There's got to be another way."

Sister Angelica touched her arm. "We can turn back to where the school is and take Orange Hill Road."

Eve looked at her in despair. "Is that the only way?"

"Yes, yes, it's the only way."

Orange Hill Road meandered inland, curving around the mountain. It passed through another small village, then turned back to Old Sugar Mill Road, way past the Plantation. They'd have to track back for miles.

It was the only way. Trying to ignore the burning muscles in her left leg, Eve put the van in reverse and managed, slipping and sliding, to turn it on the narrow road, slick with mud and water. It wasn't until they'd gone for several slow, interminable miles that she realized she wouldn't have to track back all the way to the Plantation once they were back on the main road. She could go to the Keatings' estate. It would be closer, much closer.

She felt a wave of relief. If only the rest of the road was clear! Sister Angelica was praying again, as was, she assumed, Sister Bernadette in the back seat. She hoped they were praying for the right stuff. The babies on Sister Angelica's lap, mercifully, were asleep.

The village of Amelia seemed as deserted as was Ginger Bay. Eve felt an eerie sense of being all alone in an empty, hostile world. The road was narrower and harder to negotiate. She felt tired and tense and her neck and shoulders ached from the exertion. The rain went on and on, not letting up. The road went on and on and on. She was on automatic now, not feeling, not thinking, just clutching the wheel, staring into the dark—going, going.

Finally, the turnoff on to Old Sugar Mill Road. There was a stop sign. She gritted her teeth and pushed her left foot down on the clutch, shifted down and came to a stop. She might have eased around the corner without stopping, but it was a sharp turn and she'd have to shift down to first gear anyway to do it safely on the narrow, wet road. Putting the gear in neutral, she released her foot from the clutch. She took in a deep breath, shook her arms and moved her head around to relax her neck muscles. Once more she worked the clutch and made a right turn toward Cinnamon Bay Estate. Only two more miles now and they'd be safe.

Two more miles was like two hundred, and when finally she saw the lights of the house, she felt like breaking down and crying like a baby.

But of course she did not. She drove slowly up the long drive and came to a stop near the front door. She crawled out, staggered to the door and knocked.

After that she wasn't sure what happened. Only that there was all sorts of commotion and the children were crying again.

Then she was out herself, back to the van, helping to get them all out. Her leg ached and she could barely hold herself up in the power of the wind that bit into her face. A twig swept into her face and she felt the pain just above her left eye.

She was holding the last child by the hand when car lights swept up the drive. A man jumped out as the car came to a stop, and there was Parker, striding up to her, wet hair plastered against his face.

"Eve? Thank God! Are you all right?" He looked half crazed with his wild eyes and sodden clothes. "You're bleeding!"

Eve wiped her face. It was sticky with mud and dirt. She looked at her hand; there was blood on it. She stared at it. "I guess I got hurt. I don't know."

One of the servants came rushing out, took the child and rushed back indoors. Parker put his arm around her and helped her inside, closing the door.

It was dry inside, and light. So much light. She sagged against him.

"Why didn't you ask for help?" he asked. "For God's sake, Eve, why didn't you ask for help?"

"Nobody would have given it to me. They'd keep me from going out, don't you see? It was already storming and raining." She sighed. "How did you know I was here?"

He groaned. "The manager told me he couldn't find you. We looked all over for you. Then we found the van missing." He closed his eyes. "I went out to look for you at the orphanage."

"You couldn't get there!"

"I know. I turned around and went through Amelia. Then I found the papaya tree across the road. I walked the rest of the way. The house..." He closed his eyes.

"The house what?"

"A tree fell on the roof and the whole front caved in. Glass everywhere."

"Oh, my God!" I was right, she thought, I knew something terrible was going to happen if I didn't get out of the house.

"Nobody was there." Parker's voice was toneless now. "I knew you were out there somewhere. I knew you would have had to walk to the tree with all those kids, get back into the van. I knew you'd have come through Amelia. You weren't anywhere on the road. I thought you might have come here." He hauled her against him. "Oh, God," he groaned, "I thought I was going crazy!"

Eve leaned heavily against him. Her left leg wouldn't take any more weight. She felt like a rag doll without bones.

"Why did you do it, Eve?" he went on. "How did you get it in your crazy little head to go out there in the middle of a storm?"

Her cheek rested against his shoulder and she closed her eyes. "I was afraid the hurricane would hit us head-on. I knew it would blow the orphanage away—I could feel it in my bones."

"This is not the center of the hurricane, Eve! It's out at sea. It's just the outer fringes hitting us. That's what they've been saying all along!"

She sighed, utterly weary, and lifted her face to look at him. "I just had to go. I knew something terrible was going to happen if I didn't go there." Tears of fatigue and shock began to run down her cheeks.

"Oh, God," he groaned. "Look at you!"

She ran a hand through her hair, then caught her reflection in the beveled mirror on the entryway hall. Speechlessly she stared at herself. Streaks of blood and mud ran over her face. Her hair was plastered to her head and her T-shirt clung wetly to her breasts. She turned away, and he tightened his arms around her.

"Eve," he said, his voice choked, "you're the most beautiful woman in the world, you know that?"

She gave a hysterical little laugh. It changed into a dry sob.

Fiona came into the hall. "Parker? Eve? What are you doing here in the hall? Come on in, get some dry clothes on, for Pete's sake!"

They followed her into the large kitchen. Eve's legs were shaking so hard, Parker had to help her.

"How's your leg?" he asked.

"It hurts." She began to shiver.

Parker pushed her down on a chair and David handed her a glass. "Here, some brandy to revive you."

Eve drank it down, wincing as the brandy burned going down. "Where are the kids?"

"In one of the upstairs bedrooms. They're getting washed and dried. They've had something to drink already. We'll get some food on the table here in a minute."

Eve wiped at her face with her hand. "I'd better get myself cleaned up too. Oh, Fiona, I'm sorry to do this to you."

Fiona laughed. "Don't be an idiot!" She was helping the cook at the counter, slicing bread and cheese and cutting a meat pie into wedges. "What in God's name made you do this? It's only a storm. They would have been perfectly safe at the orphanage."

"They wouldn't," said Parker. "I was there when I went looking for her. A tree fell on the house and the whole front of it's caved in."

Fiona's hand stilled. "Oh, no!" she whispered. She stared at Eve, wide-eyed. With a trembling hand, Eve picked up her brandy and took another drink.

Parker put his glass down. "If she hadn't got them out, it would have been a disaster."

Fiona lowered her knife. "Oh, Eve, how did you know?"

"I didn't—not about the tree. I was just afraid the hurricane would change course and hit head-on. I had this terrible feeling I had to get those kids out of that house. I can't explain it any other way."

Suddenly the kitchen was filled with noise. The nuns, dressed in flowered bathrobes, were bringing in the children, all dry, dressed in a strange assortment of clothes. The fear was washed from their faces along with the dirt, eyes lighting up as they noticed the food on the table.

A servant girl took Parker and Eve upstairs to another one of the spare bedrooms. Without Parker's help, Eve wouldn't have been able to make it up the stairs. He put her down on the big bed. Two bathrobes and two large blue towels, both a matching blue, lay at the foot end.

"You go first," said Parker, pointing at the bathroom. "I'll run the bath."

Eve didn't argue. "Okay."

She sat on the bed, not able to move. Her strength was gone. Silent tears began to drip down her cheeks. She didn't know why she was crying. The children were safe. She was safe. Everything was fine. There was no reason to cry.

Parker came out of the bathroom, knelt down by the bed and took her in his arms. "Oh, Eve," he said huskily. "Come on, let me help you."

She didn't protest as he began to take off her muddy, sodden sneakers, her T-shirt and bra, then her jeans and panties. Everything was sopping wet, sticking to her skin. She shivered, and she didn't know if it was the shock, or the touch of his hands on her bare skin, or both.

He wrapped one of the robes around her and helped her into the bathroom and into the bath, which was full of sudsy, scented water. The warmth of the water was like a balm for her tired, aching muscles, soothing the tension out of her. She lay back and closed her eyes.

"I'll help you," Parker said again. He washed the mud and blood from her face, shampooed her hair. She felt like a child, but she was beyond caring.

"You want to stay in for a while?" he asked.

She shook her head. "I'd better not—I'd probably fall asleep." Besides, he needed to get in too. She got up and he helped her get out of the tub.

She caught sight of herself in the full-length mirror. There was a cut above her eye. It was swollen a little, but it had already stopped bleeding. There were other scratches and bruises on face and arms. She looked like hell.

She met Parker's eyes in the mirror and flushed. She felt suddenly self-conscious standing there naked in front of him—she wasn't sure why. She sat down on a stool and took the towel out of his hands. "I can do it," she said. She began to dry her face and arms and shoulders, aware of him watching her, mouth curving in a smile.

"You're feeling better," he stated.

"Yes, much, thank you."

He helped her put on the robe. Holding on to him, she hobbled over to the bed and sat down. He got another towel and squeezed the water out of her hair.

"You go now," she said. "I'll be all right."

He took the other towel and robe and disappeared into the bathroom, leaving the door open a crack. It made her smile.

She was beginning to feel better. She limped over to the dressing table and sat down in front of the mirror. She was squeezing the water out of her hair when she heard the knock on the door. She got up to open it, finding the girl who had taken them up earlier, looking uncomfortable.

"Mrs. Keating says I bring you to this room, but Mr. Adams, he have another one. I am sorry—I think you are married."

Eve smiled at her. "That's all right. Don't worry about it—I'll tell him. He's in the shower now."

"Thank you." The girl went away down the hall and Eve closed the door.

"Who was that?" Parker stood in the bathroom door, wrapped in an identical blue bathrobe.

"The girl who took us up here." Eve sat down on the stool again, feeling a little dizzy. "She made a mistake. You're supposed to be in another room."

"No, I'm not," he said calmly. "I'm right here where I belong." He came toward her, tossing his damp towel on the bed. He lifted her off the stool, drawing her close against him. "I love you, Eve."

Her throat closed and tears flooded her eyes. "I love you too," she whispered.

"I've been a blind, stupid fool," he went on, his voice husky with emotion. "You were right all along about my not forgiving you. After you walked out, it was all I could think of. I was stuck in the past and I was wrong." He tightened his arms around her. "I love you, Eve. I love who you are, what you are. I need you."

Her tongue wouldn't move. She could only stand there in his arms, her face against the warmth of his neck, feeling as if some giant cloud had lifted and everything inside her was light and warm and joyous.

"Tonight I went crazy when I couldn't find you. I don't want to do without you, Eve, not ever again." He eased his hold on her and looked down into her face. "Let's get married," he said softly. "Let's make everything right."

Eve bit her lip and nodded, relief, sweet and light, filling her being. "Yes."

His arms tightened around her. "I'll be doing a lot of commuting," he said. "Do you have any idea how long it will be before you'll be back in Philadelphia?"

"Not too long." She smiled up at him. "My father has taken charge." She told him about the official Government request that had gone out to Washington.

"Good, great. If anyone can help things along, your father can."

"I thought you wanted my father to mind his own business," she said, smiling sweetly.

"Don't argue," he said, and kissed her, a long, passionate kiss. "It's going to be hard for me not to have you with me right away, you know."

"I know."

"So when shall we get married?" he asked.

"Today, tomorrow. Here."

He laughed. "That won't give us much time to plan the wedding."

"I did that once," smiled Eve. "I'm not doing it again." An image flashed in her mind—Elsa in her short white dress and John in his flowered shirt in front of the little church with Father Matthias.

He chuckled. "Where's your father?"

"In Sydney."

"I don't think he'll make it. You're not thinking of getting married without him, are you?"

She shifted in his arms and sighed. "No. I guess we'll have to wait until we can gather the troops—your parents, Joshua's family, my father, my friend Sophie and my friends here. Anyone else you want to be there?"

He gave her an odd look. "Is that all?"

"More won't fit into the Ark of Love Church."

"You're serious about wanting to get married here?"

Eve nodded. "Father Matthias can do it." She smiled, thinking of him. How many times had he asked her if there was anything he could do for her? Now she knew.

She thought of the wedding she'd once planned in the beautiful church in Philadelphia with the tall, handsome minister with his richly modulated voice who would perform the ceremony. She thought of all the years of Sundays she had sat in the gleaming church with her father and grandmother and of all the sermons that had never reached into her spoiled little soul.

She thought of Father Matthias, short and bald, and the tiny little church with its leaking roof and rickety pews. She thought of him praying with the children, hugging them, telling them stories. Love. In the end it was the only thing that mattered.

"It will be perfect," she said.

JAYNE ANN KRENTZ

A two-part epic tale from one of today's most popular romance novelists!

Dreams
Parts One & Two

The warrior died at her feet, his blood running out of the cave entrance and mingling with the waterfall. With his last breath he cursed the woman— told her that her spirit would remain chained in the cave forever until a child was created and born there....

So goes the ancient legend of the Chained Lady and the curse that bound her throughout the ages—until destiny brought Diana Prentice and Colby Savager together under the influence of forces beyond their understanding. Suddenly they were both haunted by dreams that linked past and present, while their waking hours were filled with danger. Only when Colby, Diana's modern-day warrior, learned to love, could those dark forces be vanquished. Only then could Diana set the Chained Lady free....

WELCOME TO

The quintessential small town, where everyone knows everybody else!

Finally, books that capture the pleasure of tuning in to your favorite TV show!

GREAT READING...GREAT SAVINGS...AND A FABULOUS FREE GIFT!

Each book set in Tyler is a self-contained love story; together, the twelve novels stitch the fabric of the community. The covers honor the old American tradition of quilting; each cover depicts a patch of the large Tyler quilt.

With Tyler you can receive a fabulous gift, ABSOLUTELY FREE, by collecting proofs-of-purchase found in each Tyler book. And use our special Tyler coupons to save on your next TYLER book purchase.

Join your friends at Tyler for the seventh book, ARROWPOINT by Suzanne Ellison, available in September.

Rumors fly about the death at the old lodge! What happens when Renata Meyer finds an ancient Indian sitting cross-legged on her lawn?

If you missed *Whirlwind* (March), *Bright Hopes* (April), *Wisconsin Wedding* (May), *Monkey Wrench* (June), *Blazing Star* (July) or *Sunshine* (August) and would like to order them, send your name, address, zip or postal code, along with a check or money order for $3.99 for each book ordered (please do not send cash), plus 75¢ postage and handling ($1.00 in Canada), payable to Harlequin Reader Service, to:

In the U.S.
3010 Walden Avenue
P.O. Box 1325
Buffalo, NY 14269-1325

In Canada
P.O. Box 609
Fort Erie, Ontario
L2A 5X3

Please specify book title(s) with your order.
Canadian residents add applicable federal and provincial taxes.

TYLER-7